The Notebooks of Michael Mabius

A Novel by

Elia Katz

ISBN: 978-0-6151-5690-3

Published by West Hollywood Books

To contact the Author or West Hollywood Books email:
Jake3146@yahoo.com

Prologue

Susan –

I am sending you all the notebooks, written by Michael, concerning the last days of his life, exactly as he sent them to me. When you read them, you'll notice that he addresses me by name somewhere toward the end once or twice. I don't think, however, that he meant to write all of this for me. I seem to have been an afterthought, or some such thing. I have no idea why he wrote any of it, actually, or why he chose to dwell so much on those aspects of his life that all who loved him, as we did, will agree led to his destruction, but these were his choices. Susan – you may have been the cause of these books. It looks like he started the first notebook around the time you returned to New York, and you were on his mind, and then he saw you again...

The choice of what should be done with this, and of who should see it, I leave to you. I have kept a xerox for myself, and sent one to his father, of course.

By the way, don't be taken in by all that overpouring of emotionality in July. They say at the end he never spoke except to bite somebody's head off.

My love to your growing family.

-- Jack

Book I.

May 8. Tuesday. 5:03 A.M.

A xerox of the shroud of Turin is taped to the wall above the non-working and not decorative fireplace. An ambulance siren travels across fifteenth street, from 6th Ave., heading for 7th, not turning. Why not? It's stopping one block away.

I have just returned from the living room, where I looked out the window for the ambulance. Saw nothing but beautiful trees, leaves, fences, red window panes filled with sunbeams across the street. Breathed.

I would like to write a book, to save myself, as soon as possible. I have to think of it, do it, finish it, get it typed.

After I do it, I don't care what happens. I will happily give up. But just once, starting now, at 5:12, let me make that effort I have always known I must finally make - or not be myself - the one effort that represents the victory of my former ambitions, formed in the heart of a young child, for no known reason and therefore, I believe, pure, honest and powerful, over my present constraints, dependencies, and general weakness.

6:17 A.M.

Ate instant waffles.

6:22 - 6:23 - 6:24

Looking at the digits fall. AM. PM. White numerals on little black cards, the cards divided latitudinally in their middles - The mechanism starts to whirr about 45 seconds after the minute has begun. It whirrs until it clicks, clears its throat, then exerts the sigh of great effort toward which all its whirring has been leading - it pushes the next black card up, drops the old minute into the dead pile beneath visibility and drops the new minute into view. This time of night, when there are no other sounds, except the occasional garbage truck, the gears of the clock, though soft, fill all the space of hearing.

I have returned to the city of my birth, after six years away in the West, and now I have been here one full year, and this is the closing of the second year here. My 32nd, or 31st birthday soon approaches. When I left this city, I had so much, I didn't even need hope. When I came back, I had hope but not much else. Currently, I feel much excitement, but none of it pointed. Not that it worries me. I was looking for a vacation from hope.

Weds. May 9. 5:44 A.M.

There is talking in the courtyard. The digital clock clicks off another minute. The sky has light but no color. The *I Ching* is resting at the head of the bed, after several gruelling hours of my importuning. I am reading *Tropic of Cancer*, and it occurred to me last night on the way from the University Bar to the Blue Parrot, that Henry Miller, like Jack Kerouac, does the kind of writing that should be done. Just write whatever is going on, and forget it.

I am unable to go to sleep. I'm afraid of going to the dentist tomorrow.

Interesting, if frustrating, encounter with the *I Ching* this evening ... Pressed down with despair about the fate of *"I Track Down Freaks"* just having lost the agent for that book because of something the *I Ching* told me to do, I said to it: "Are all your pieces of advice about my book leading toward its ultimately being published?" to which it answered, "No." That sent a chill down my spine. I've been relying on this *I Ching* creature for every action taken in regard to the final draft, the xeroxing of the manuscript, who to send it to, when to mail it, whether or not to call this or that person to find out if he's read it yet - and on & on -

I tried to remain calm. I have, in the past, become so angry at the *I Ching* that I have thrown it across the room, or out the window, or spit on it - tearing the pages out and jumping on them, or setting pages on fire, then asking "What do you think of *that*, Fuckhead?" ... However, I had resolved never to do anything like that again, always to remain calm, realizing that the paradoxical answers of the *I Ching* would ultimately resolve themselves to me. Most, in the past, have. Although not all. There are a number of former answers of the *Ching's* I still remember - some after years - as having been totally wrong - and having cost me something. I am still brooding over some old betrayals. "Who are you? Who is speaking through these coins?" Are they spirits, demons? God Himself, hiding, yet speaking? Are the answers it gives derived from my own brain, or is there a Being who is the entire air, every molecule, that turns the coins one way or the other, answering every question, while at the same time entering every creature on earth who inhales?

I talked to Susan few nights ago, when Tracy called her from here. Naturally, I can't stop thinking about our talk. She sounded sad, or at least I thought she did. But I didn't ask her about it. I told her Tracy and I were watching TV, a show about the "Temple System" of irrigating the rice fields of Bali. She interrupted me, saying "Do you think we'll see each other?"

The way she said it brought all of my blood to my face instantaneously, and made it impossible for me to answer right away. I said, "Uhh," when I realized I had been silent too long, and I looked over at Tracy, who was beside me on the mattress, but leaning attentively toward the little color television that sits here by the head of my floor-level bed, on a cardboard box containing the publisher's overstock of the paperback edition of my last book, with her chin on her fist, watching the endlessly fascinating story (I have seen this show many times before) of those irrigation ditches in Bali, that are alternately flooded and drained by a system of gates, each gate controlled by a priest, and located either within, or right beside, a temple. Tracy was watching the part about that festival they have designed to appease the god of the volcano. When I was again able to croak out hesitant speech, I said to Susan: "How's Ben?"

"Searching," she said.

Ben is her husband. He's searching for a job.

I said, "Did he try Mirthco? Did you tell him what I said?"

"Well, he called your friend James. But your friend told him they weren't actually looking for any new writers."

"Oh, well..." I said, "But what about..."

"Story editor?"

"Right. Did he ask about the possibility of a job as a story editor?"

"Well, yes, he did mention it, but I mean you must have known your friend *James* is the story editor. Didn't you?"

"Oh, is that what they call him?"

"It is, yes." She paused for a long time, and I could tell she was taking a long drag on a cigarette. Then she said, "Ben feels you set him up."

"I was trying to *help* him."

"Well, I told him he was crazy, but he says you must have known this James..."

"I didn't, though."

"Let's talk about something else," said Susan.

"I'm very sorry about this," I said.

"Well," she said, in a tone that indicated she did not entirely believe what I was saying. Then she said, "He thinks you did it because you're still in love with me."

To which I replied in exasperation (but with an eye toward a better future) "But doesn't that mean I want you to be *happy*? Doesn't that mean I want your husband to be employed, so he will not cause you to have to go out to work as a cook?"

"A chef," she said. "Well, anyway, let me talk to Tracy."

I put Tracy on the phone. Then I crawled over her so I could be up next to the TV while Tracy and Susan talked.

Tracy now began a long series of denials. "No, no ... no ... ah, no ... uh-uh ... no really, no ... well, but no..." and so on. "No, we're just watching this show," and so on and so forth.

Finally, she reached over me and put the phone between its plastic trapezoids, and said "Sheesh!" in her just-above-a-whisper high-pitched voice. "She wanted to know if we were sleeping together."

"What did you tell her?" I switched the channel to a movie called *Morituri*, starring Marlon Brando and Trevor Howard.

"I told her she was crazy, naturally," said Tracy. Her voice is really *not* a whisper - her words have all the qualities of words that might come from any other woman's mouth - musicality, inflection, graceful modifications among an enormously wide range of emotional colorations - but all at such a low *volume* that sometimes I have the feeling I'm hearing a voice trapped under some heavy stone I happen to be passing, a voice calling out: "Here I am ... over here!" This unwillingness on her part to impose in any way the sound of her voice, bothers some people, but I like it. It makes you listen to her very carefully. It makes you lean toward her, sometimes even touching one of her arms, in the hope that this extra contact will cause vibrations that pass through her veins when she speaks to add a few words to your comprehension of what she is saying.

"Anyway," she said, "What would give her that idea? Did you say anything to her?"

"No, of course I didn't. Only could have originated with Arianna."

"Oh, you told *her*," said Tracy, raising herself from the mattress with a single motion, and padding over to the closet to look through my pockets after first patting them all on both sides.

"No, I denied it, but you know how she is. And of course, she's good friends with Ben."

Tracy pulled the rectangular, beatup pouch of aluminum foil from the pocket of my tired corduroy jacket, where I keep it hidden from my three apartment-mates, and padded back over here, to the mattress-area, with a cute look on her face.

Was the sun still in the sky at that time?

Was the room washed in afternoon red, evening blue haze, or what? I can't remember. I think the news came on, and that's the last thing I recall, until...

...I woke up and it was dark. Hours had passed. The candle was flickering in a pool of wax down in the saucer where it had stood. I was aware of someone standing above me, looking at me. I opened my eyes, expecting to see Tracy, but it was Susan. She was holding her dark hair back behind her ears with her fingers so it wouldn't fall over her face as she looked downward, and she was smiling. There was light from the courtyard coming through the window at the head of the bed, and the way it caught the glistening of Susan's eyes, I thought she might have been crying. However, before I could ask her about it, or say anything, I saw her start to check around the edge of the mattress, trying to work out some way of sitting down without falling. I put my hand up to give her something to lean on as she sat down.

"Well, well! Taking a nap?" she said in a slightly mocking tone. Then she looked around the room (I was grateful she had not turned on the light) and she said, "This is worse than I imagined!" After a second or two, she managed to stretch and turn her back in such a way as to be able to reach me, and place a kiss on my cheek. I said, "Susan - I can't believe it!"

She said, looking serious, "I just thought if we could talk..."

"Sure," I said.

She looked at me in a very sweet way. Too nostalgic, too peaceful for me - because from the instant I saw her, all the emotions of a *present* and overwhelming passionate involvement, had returned to me. But then she looked at me in a more intense way, and seemed troubled, though I had not caused any trouble, so far, and she said my name, and we kissed, very softly, and I tasted the salt tears on her lightly lipsticked upper lip, and I saw the flushed quality of her face. She said, "*One* of the things I think we'd better talk about is these conversations we've been having on the phone..."

"Have I said anything I shouldn't have said?"

"You *have* made it pretty clear that you'd like us to be together again."

She looked at me, but I didn't say anything.

She said, "And all these *people* telling me 'Michael still loves you, Michael still loves you...' How do they get that impression?"

I mumbled in a shame-faced, down-in-the-mouth way, "I don't know," but I knew what she was talking about.

She said, "You must know there's no possibility for us. I'm married."

"I know that."

"Good, then," she said.

We stared at each other a long time, and finally I said, "I thought the reason you came down to New York, was because you wanted to see me." Pause. "I mean, at least partly."

She shook her head. "No. That wasn't it. It was - well, as you've probably heard from Tracy - I sent Ben down here to look for a job, and that was over two months ago, and he wanted to see me. And I -" She let go of my hand and picked up her cigarette. " - I feel I haven't been *fair* to him, exactly."

"What does that mean?"

"Oh, it doesn't matter. It's just one of those thoughts I get when I spend too much time thinking."

"And what does *that* mean?"

"And anyway," she said, ignoring my questions, "I just got tired of sitting around in that place all by myself in the middle of the winter. I mean, *you* know what it's like out there during the winter..."

She was referring me to the recollection of a winter we two once spent together, on Provincetown. We smoked a joint, and then she said she was going to work. She said, "Come see me at work, we can talk during my break." Then, she left. I was still half asleep, but my heart was crashing around from my stomach to my skull.

Later, I walked the mile or so to the restaurant where Susan is working. She was just finishing up for the night. I was surprised to see her going into the kitchen, through the wet green doors, carrying a large, heavy tray full of dishes. She had mentioned that sometimes very late she helped the waitresses with their tables, but I had not pictured her as carrying anything heavier than a few coffee cups or pastry plates. But now, seeing her in this dark place, that smelled slightly of beer, and was too warm, too low-ceilinged, too red-and-white - I didn't like it at all. Her arms were bare and I saw for the first time a *change* in Susan's appearance, from the way she was when we were together. Her arms were lean and muscular - tight with strength. She is tan, and obviously in very good physical condition - but those strong arms bothered me...

When she was finished working, she said goodbye to the other people who worked there, and some of the patrons, who evidently knew her, and protested when they learned she would not be joining them at their table for a drink. One of them - a baby-faced fifty year old man - told her that the man sitting to his right was the heir to the throne of Italy, and that "even now" loyalists in and out of Italy were preparing the way for his return to power. The man who had been indicated looked at Susan sheepishly and grinned. "When I am king, you sit with me," he said, and the other one said, "Italy's been a *shit*hole without *Claud*io on the throne!" I sat with these men, drinking black cherry soda, while Susan got her stuff. She came back with her jacket on - a silky bomber jacket - and we went to a bar she knew, and sat in the back room.

I said, "I didn't like the looks of that tray you were carrying."

She said, "What tray?"

"At *work*. I mean, I thought you had a cinch job. Now it turns out you have to carry loads around that would fell a horse!"

"Oh, now," she said, but I could tell she was tired, too tired even to pretend it wasn't true.

After a while I asked if she was happy in her marriage. She said, "Yes, I would say that I am, all things considered." I don't want to write about this. I don't want to think off all the years I could have been beside her, but I've been alone.

I walked her home. We kissed, and she allowed herself to press close to me. Then, we were standing there looking at each other when around the corner, half a block away, two people wheeled into view. Her eyes shifted in their direction, and she squinted to see far into the night illumination. I could feel the muscles of her body tense up when she thought she recognized one of the people. "I have to go," she said, and moved against the wall, to a place where my body shielded her from the vision of those people.

I said, "What's the difference if anyone sees us? If we still love each other, we should be together. We should be married."

"Michael," she said rather quickly, and with a tone of tired finality in her voice, "I came to see you before, because I've been unhappy, very unhappy, and it was so wonderful talking to you on the phone those times, and I hoped - I mean just *may*be I was hoping - praying, if you want to know the truth - that somehow it *would* be possible, but now I know it's hopeless. I knew it when I was in your room."

"What are you talking about?" I said, but I already knew.

"When I saw what you have there. You know what I mean."

"No."

"The dope. The needle."

I didn't say anything.

"Goodbye, darling," she said. She touched the side of my face, then quickly looked past me, down the street, across which a slight wind was blowing a cardboard box, to watch the two men she had seen before. They were talking in the doorway of a closed store. Then she turned and went down the dark side-street the few steps to her building's entrance, her hands pushed down in the pockets of her bomber-jacket, looking down at the street, and she pushed the door open with her shoulder, looked back at me one more time, her face already halfway hidden by the edges of the bricks, and then she was gone.

Weds. May 9. 2:02 P.M.

After two weeks of cool weather, it is 90°. All the windows are open, making the existence of a live, practicing drummer across the courtyard all the more noticeable. It's almost time to get high, although in a perfect world I wouldn't get high until 6 o'clock. Ralph Hornblower called today, in response to the message I left on his machine. He said he was terribly sorry he lost me my *I Track Down Freaks* agent thru this "imbroglio" but *he* won't agent the book unless I make certain changes first.

"But Ralph." I said in the voice of a man unnaturally suppressing his rage, "You *lost* me my agent! I had a perfectly good agent for that book until he learned from an editor at Putnam's that *another agent* was sending the book around too. Naturally, when he heard that, he thought *I* had *given* it to another agent, and he wrote me a very angry letter, and said he was discontinuing our professional relationship. I don't blame him. I would have thought the same thing. But the fact is; I *didn't* give it to another agent to send around. You sent it around without telling me. *You* lost me my agent. How can you now refuse to represent the book yourself? Is that moral?"

He laughed in a weird, appreciative way, as though I were making fun of myself and he was a good audience. He's not taking this "moral" stuff too seriously.

"Well," he said, "I *said* I was sorry. I was only trying to help. I happen to be a friend of Marge Stern at Putnam's and I thought she might get a kick out of the book, so I sent it to her. Besides, I felt a little responsible because I was the one who originally bought it when I was still an editor and you wouldn't be having to look for a new publisher if I hadn't left to go out on my own, and become ... an agent. So sue me. The fact remains, Marge had several criticisms, which *I* took very much to heart, and as it stands *now*, no, I would not be able to send it around as it is now written. It needs *extensive* rewriting, I'm afraid. Not that it isn't *fine* the way it is. It's just that it's such a god damn tough *sell*. Whereas, if you could make the book a bit more ... commercial, which would not be hard to do ... more dialog, strengthen the love story, don't *tell* the reader the main character is dead and resurrected *quite* so early in the story ... things like that ... and I'm sure I could get a *good* advance for it. But you have to be willing to work!"

Now I have no agent, and the necessity of doing revisions to *get* an agent, all because he was trying to do me a favor.

Luckily, the *I Ching* put me on my guard against rash acts, or I would have told him I'd kill him if he didn't find me a publisher. Instead, I was very pleasant, asked him to call Putnam's and explain, so it will get back to the other agent, the real agent, that it was not my fault, that he, Hornblower, took it upon himself to send my book to a publisher without telling me about it - and maybe if he learns that, he'll take me back.

However, I do think I will have to change at least the *order* of the first 30 pages. Start with Cade waking up in the morning, heating his back on the radiator to revive himself; *then* go to the story of The Cyclops Child, *then* to Cade killing the Cyclops Child.

It's the only thing that makes sense, if you can call it sense.

Darling, I will shower
You with taxing power
If you will consent
To join my government.

Weds. May 9. 6:52 P.M.

Tracy called this morning to say she would be in the neighborhood this afternoon, did I want to have lunch. I used the dentist as an excuse to back out. Then I didn't go to the dentist, and didn't call him either. I'm sure I'll regret that bit of rebelliousness very soon. As for Tracy - she's quite promiscuous for a girl of 22. A casual inquisition into her average sex habits brought forth a river of names, nations, occupations - was Susan like that, too? With Tracy, it's the President of Time-Life, the director of the Met - with Robin it's stunt men and actors.

Weds. May 9.

Lenny was just here with his friend Glenn. Glenn is a writer for various magazines, and he has his own T.V. show which is on late at night, one of those shows where the lights periodically swoon and fall, casting the screen in long shadows - He seems like a very nice guy - very quiet, a little nervous, precise. He seemed to like conversation not at all - therefore it was pleasant to converse with him. He is writing an article about "the homosexual substructure of all pornography." The male reader identifies with the female character in the book, or the naked girl in the nudie magazines.

8:16, and not dark yet! This daylight savings is a pain in the ass.

What to do?

Eat? No.

Wait for the call from my dealer, then run to the Citibank cash dispenser, bring him the money, then wait some more, while he drags around visiting his musical friends and otherwise wasting my time?

Yes, I better wait.

Sammy! the last time I called, you had a different message on your answering machine. That means you've been home & heard your messages. Yet, you have not called yr. old pal.

How long do you think I'm going to stand for this crap? I give you all my money, that I earn writing dialogue for rats to exchange, and this is how you pay me back.

Ah, here comes the true night, at last! Spread that blueberry jam! There goes the depthful outside world, blinking out. Soon the catatonics across the street will realize night has finally come, and will start putting on their lights.

I should go eat.

But what?

Not meat. It's too hot. All I want is pancakes. For 3 weeks, all I've eaten has been pancakes. With syrup - no sausages, ham or bacon - why bother with the deceit of protein? If I want a salty taste I'll get extra butter and smash three or four pats on the cold pancakes.

Now, don't excite yrself with food images or you won't be able to wait for Sam's all-important call. Be calm. A rat will press a little lever several hundred times for food, but he'll press the little lever until he dies if he thinks he'll be rewarded with heroin. These are the facts science gives us to help us cope with our mysterious lives and errors. Thank you, torturers of rats, for this quantitative measure of how long you will continue forcing rats to press levers.

I press the seven little buttons of Sam's phone number again and again... Each time, I am treated to a few bars of punk-rock music - whatever band he is trying to push this week, followed by the sound of his message to his many callers: "This is 6942. I've gone out for dinner, I should be back pretty soon, so just *leave* your number, and the *time* you called, and I *will* get back to you." Most of the time I hang up.

Weds. May 9. 11:04 P.M.

Talked to Sam. He won't tumble tonight. He has a guest he must entertain for his record company.

I had pancakes at *The Chariot.* The women in the street were beautiful. If it wasn't so muggy I would have turned around and followed a certain tall one who looked at me lingeringly. She had a nice face, and she was eating Italian ices.

The *I Ching* says I'll meet a new girl within a week. If I interpret it correctly. It's tricky on the subject of women. Sometimes I think it doesn't want me to find one - that it wants me to stay in solitude, so I will be forced, out of boredom, to spend hour after hour asking the Book - as I do, questions about every realm into which the image-making insects of all my forms of greed take me.

With whom do I speak as often as I speak with you, *Ching*? If I may be overly familiar, forgetting the path of the golden mean.

Newsflash...

... Just talked to Sam. He will not go. His client from Canada *is* in town! He is going to the Mudd Club to see Screamin' Jay Hawkins. Did I want to go? I wanted to force him at gunpoint to go on my errand first! The reason is, I must absolutely write five to seven pages of rat dialog tonight before sleep, and I will not be capable of doing that without at least $50 worth of heroin.

Should I try Robin?

I'll ask...
I think the answer is "No."
Just the way I see it.
Too much trouble.
For methadone biscuits - which is all she has.
Keep thinking.

Look at the way those three pairs of shoes seem to be walking across the floor, toward the Entertainment Section of the *NY Times*. They look like the The History of Mankind, for some reason.

Whenever I buy a hardback book, the check with which I buy it bounces. So, this has become one of my personal mysteries. Another is the fact that whenever I see a person I haven't seen for a few years, that person is pre-figured. Like the day before, or two days before, I'll see someone in the street who I *think* is that person. Now, if I see someone I think is George Massenburg, I know in a couple of days I *will* see George Massenburg.

In college, I did a terrible thing - going to parties and dances too soon after the death of my Grandfather, looking for girls. I couldn't stop myself. I wasn't in a fraternity, but they used to let us come to their parties, Jack and me. At one of these parties, I saw a girl I thought I knew. She was looking straight at me, with a friendly smile on her face. This, it turned out, was because she had thought she recognized me. She thought I was a boy named Ian, and she called me Ian for several days afterwards.

We danced together once, for almost the last time in the next five years, and then I asked her to leave with me. She said where to. We went to my apartment where we kicked in the window together, because Jack's brother had locked himself in. Once inside, she pulled out some grass. I said, "what do you need that for?" Which is funny now that I think of it... I didn't realize until several years later how favorably my reaction impressed her. I lectured her about the futility of the search for Happiness by any route, since it was illusory. I don't remember what I said. I remember smoking her pipe with her. That affected my brain and I started reading to her aloud from the many piles of paper covered with my scrawling. I didn't want her to think I was only interested in sex. She was the most beautiful girl I had ever seen. I was in love with her.

The next day, I called her to ask if I could see her again. According to her recollection, I told her I was Superman, but I don't remember that. I went to her house, because her parents wanted to meet me. I had invited her to dinner, but when she appeared in her parents' living room, she had a set of pots & pans, and the ingredients of an apple pie. I couldn't believe my good fortune. As soon as we left the house, and were walking toward the bus stop, I said I loved her. She said, "I'm glad you said that first." Now, she doesn't remember saying that, or won't admit it. It upsets her to think she said that, the way things turned out ... dot dot dot ...

"I've been abused
and false accused
so many times
for things I know
I didn't do
But I know
one day soon
it will all be over
and I'll go to heaven
and I'll get my crown."

So sing the gospel singers on the radio ... now they're done... Now we hear:

"But I learned to trust Him
Since He changed me
He changed me
He changed me
God He changed me
Listen!
He changed me
I'm glad!
He changed me

Created!
He changed me
A Clean Heart!
Changed me
A new spirit
Changed me
Changed my name!
Changed me
OWW! OWW! OWW!
Hallelujah!"
"Yes, yes! Tell him all about it ..."
Tell Jesus
Tell him
Tell Jesus
You may be
burdened
down
Tell Jesus
I know you
wanna
tell
Tell Jesus"

Dot Dot Dot ... I loved her. Tell *Him* that. He knows. He knows also what I did, what I did to her. He knows also, as my own Heart did not, but as it does now, how true my Heart would prove, over the long pay-out of the destitute, damned, fallen years, to be. As true as gold at the bottom of the sea.

Recently, I went to Texas, for some reason, and stayed in a hotel. When I left, I left a notebook behind, in which I had been writing about her. When I got back home, the notebook was waiting for me, with a note from the maid who found it while cleaning the room, saying she had read the pages I wrote in it, apologizing, but adding, "I was so moved by the tenderness of your sentiment for Susan that I felt not only must I send you back your book, instead of turning it in to the Lost-and-Found, as we are supposed to do, but I also must write you this letter, to say that I will be praying for your re-unification with your Susan ..."

There was also a letter from Susan telling me she was happy, expecting gaily her approaching marriage, but still, using a P.O. Box as a return address, although she had a real address, where she was living with her fiance. I didn't understand. Was the letter a call for help? Did she want me to rescue her from an unwise wedding? What did I still hope? Why did I want so much from her, after all those years. Move, pursue love to its most absurd degree. Make yourself appear like an idiot in the eyes of your family, her family, even the fiance's family, do not give up until the eternal gift is once again in yr. grasp -

I asked myself - Why did she write this letter to me? Only to say how happy she is; then why does she insinuate: "there is nothing to do." and "I am happy, considering I am so hard to please." Hard to please?

I did not act at that time. I let the wedding come and go without my presence, although there was a small flurry of communications between Susan and myself in the weeks leading to the ceremony. I was in California.

Shut the door, I'm digressing ... did I make that up, or hear it from somebody - James H?

Anyway, back to the Beginning - From the first sighting of her. I was in a state of grace. She was the answer to that shouting at the sky I had done on the night before I met her. Nothing else would have made me worthy of her. In the course of five years, I was to prove myself totally unworthy of her, by committing certain sins against her and against whatever living spirit may be thought to inhabit the concept, or the world - fact, of love.

I remember at the time, the idea that such a living spirit had any existence seemed meaningless to me, even though love itself didn't seem meaningless. I was very much in love with Susan, always, but it is really only since we parted - eight years ago - that, in missing her, I have come to realize what love could have meant to me, if I had possessed a sensitivity to the unbelievable (and now, unendurably absent) daily miracle of her presence. How much I meant to her. How she was able to make every place beautiful.

And another thing is how the world itself, as well as all the creatures and people in it, seemed to love both her and me, but especially her, and me because of her. The oxygen itself. Loved me better then. Everything was easy. The other thing I think of is how protective of me she was - comfortable in situations that required her to defend, stand up for, protect, or save me from any danger whatsoever. She was fearless.

For instance, one time we were at an outdoor concert which became a race riot. As we were leaving, I was hit from behind, and found myself on the ground, surrounded by a group of kids, who were screaming at me, and kicking me. Several times I felt the severe jolt of kicks in the head and neck. I had no way of getting to my feet.

Then suddenly the kicking at my head stopped. I looked straight up, from my flat position, and saw that the young man who had been kicking my head was now staggering beneath the swinging fists of none other than Susan. She had been safe on the front lawn of a house, which was on a small hill, but she had jumped from the rise of the hill onto the shoulders of the guy, and now was raining punches down on his skull while saying, "Leave him alone!"

They stopped kicking me. They stopped noticing me at all. All then began to cheer her. "Go, sister!" "You tell him!" Even the one she was hitting was happy, smiling and laughing. It was like another century from the moment just before. He seemed quite honored to have this brave, beautiful girl riding on his shoulders, beating him.

Then some of the black guys reached down to me and helped me up. They asked if I was alright. I said I was OK. They said that's good, good, as though they had just come upon the victim of a car wreck on the highway. They led me to where Susan was, now that she was standing on the ground, and said, "See, he's alright, little sister. Is that OK now?" and she said yes.

Then the one who had been jumped on by her, who had been kicking my head, and who seemed to be the leader, said, "We'll walk you out." and they walked us the few blocks to St. Paul's Avenue, where we were able to get out of the riot by going into a store.

Those guys knew it. An exceptional being. What saved my life - and hers - was not merely their response to her beauty or even her courage. Or even their delight at the absurdity of a young girl fighting that way. There was something about her that made them feel exalted, because her path had crossed theirs... They seemed to feel "If *this* person doesn't approve of us, there is something wrong with us."

I felt the black kids inspecting me, to see if I was worthy of such an angel. When they parted from us, they all said, "Take care now." and said to me, "If it wasn't for this woman you'd be dead, jack. You make her happy, now."

Susan accepted her triumph without the least momentary sign that she was surprised by it. She never even referred to it afterwards. I mean, yes, we hear about soldiers, policemen, and anarchists, all doing brave things, but the odds they face are rarely as great, and the miracles that save them are rarely as miraculous as the one that saved her and me, and still I would be surprised if any of them took his victory as much in stride, as she did, and she was just a girl in high school.

"You saved my life," I said.

"Anytime." In those days, I was protected.

About two years after that, she saved my life again. We had gone to Algeria, to take pictures as journalists. I went looking for hash, or grass or something, down a little dark street shaped like a scimitar. It curved and curved, and soon I disappeared from her sight. She was watching from a table at a cafe on the main street. I had been following two men who were supposed to lead me to what I wanted, but as soon as we were beyond the seeing of the people on the main street, they turned around, and both of them had knives. They didn't say anything, like, "Give us your money." They just walked toward me in contented silence. Soon I heard Susan's voice. I creaked my head an inch or so to the side, to see her, strolling purposefully up the street, with her arm stretched out in front of her. She called my name. "Omar has another source for the hash. Come back. Now." For some reason, the two men did not pursue me as I backed up. I later asked Susan what had made her come up the street. She had no idea, except she had a feeling I was in trouble.

I only think of her saving my life because it seems to re-assure me that there is some great plan to existence, whose whole purpose is to put us back together, finally. As though by her saving my life we have been introduced to the idea of eternal pairing, eternal bonding... There were things she did for me that were greater than saving my life.

She used to ask me to make up stories before we went to sleep, and I would try to make things up that had a certain coherency to them, so she would know I really had tried to think of a story.

Now I remember the way she walked... Now I remember being with her in the ocean... Now I remember the times she wore too much make-up. Why did that always make me feel ill?

Susan, I remember the first time I saw your form long ago. And now, I do not begrudge other men the sight of that, because I know, I am sure, that they do not see what I saw.

Because of the fact that it was created for me. And when a man looks upon the body of a woman who was created not for him, he cannot see her, not entirely, as I was able to see you. No, the other men are looking at fog, at waves of indeterminacy that pass around you like loops given over to the crowd of time, while your secret pure nakedness was only revealed to me...

Feel free to disagree.

As for myself, I prefer to think all the men who embraced you since me, have embraced you in rooms filled with smoke, fog, gloom, miasmas of blindness, inattention, and half-sleep.

At first you said you didn't want to get married, but then it turned out that wasn't true. Your parents came to visit us one time and told you I was sick. They said it wasn't my fault. My own parents' unhappy marriage had made me fearful of it. I had no model of a happy home. You told me what they said. I thought about it. They were right. I realized that in order to save you, I had to separate from you forever. The other choice was to marry, but I was sure if we did that I would ultimately desert, probably leaving you with children you would have to raise on your own, which had been the fate of my mother.

At that time, the entire meaning of "wisdom," for me, was "the avoidance of the mistakes of the parents."

I committed various sins, as a result of which my thinking lost its force. I lost my will to state myself. I had the sneaking suspicion I had entered a period of purgatorial suffering. That suspicion became a certainty after two or three years. Then I formed the idea - from where, I don't know - that I'd have to suffer for exactly seven years to pay for what I had done to Susan.

I had expected her to find a new love immediately, and to continue her life. I thought she would be much happier without me, but as the years went by, it became obvious that she was not finding happiness.

Every now and then, starting about 3 years after our final break-up, we started our pattern of long silences, punctuated by times during which we would talk to each other on the phone for hours at a time.

During these times I began to hope we could be together again, but it has not happened.

These days I have a girl named Robin, who has the same exact birthday as Susan, although she's six years younger. She also looks a little like Susan. I look for similarities - to see if they are signs of some kind. If they are, I have not been able to figure them out. However, sometimes I do suspect that Robin was sent to be almost a recapitulation of Susan, but with certain important differences.

I met Robin in Tana's Bar on Santa Monica Blvd. in Los Angeles, a hang-out for movie industry employees and she was there with two or three girl friends. I remember first peering in her direction thinking: "What a pleasant-looking, innocent-looking, radiant blonde over there, batting her gums while her slavishly attentive girlfriends ogle her beauty and glistening hair." and then returning my attention to my own girlfriend, when I thought I heard the voice of the blonde say: "God, I'd love to get *fucked* tonight!" I looked over there again and saw by the giggling fear of the other girls, and the posing of the blonde, that that was exactly what she had said. She excused herself, and walked past my table, to the rest room - telephone area, that well-known hangout-within-the-hangout. I noticed her walking, and went in that direction after her. When she came out of the ladies' room, I was at the phone, in her way. We exchanged words against the wall between the cigarette machine and the rest room doors. I put my arms around her and kissed her. Then I got back home with D. and remembered I didn't have Robin's phone number, so I took the phone into the bathroom and in whispering voice called the restaurant & described the blonde girl, so they'd bring her to the phone. As soon as I said: "Hello?" she said: "Are you talking from the bathroom?" and when I said I was she said: "You really *are* a bastard, aren't you?" but we made a date. That was 3 years ago.

Where is she tonight?

You leave her on the street when you go in to get the newspaper. You come out & there are five men circling around her like flies... Don't I deserve better treatment from you? She told me she was getting lonesome while I wrote my book on Wilhelm Reich, but I didn't think she'd do anything about it.

I light the candle on top of the TV, and think about her. I remember the time she hopped out of bed at 4 am to administer First Aid to the victims of a car crash beneath our window on Fountain Avenue. I remember last month, when she charged me $250 every two days, for $200 worth of mediocre tan heroin, because I needed it to finish my book... I remember her with that belt around her arm, that later she tied around my arm... She always seems to have a needle around the house...

May 10. 2:02 A.M.

Marty wants to get a dog. I fought it. I don't want it running around over my head or barking when they're not home to shut it up, or romping around on the stairs or in the kitchen, nor do I want to grow attached to it and have it die. Anyway, Marty and his wife deposit, I think, more than their share of filth and trash around the house without the help of a dog.

These dogs you get from the pound, especially, are prone to die on you.

I remember Lady the First. She was a little bassengee puppy we got from the pound. She died of distemper, caught at the pound. Then we got Lady II, and she was around for a long time, but ultimately she got some kind of tumor, and was in a terrible mood for the last couple of years. We had to reach in under the bureau, where she hid, and pull her out by force to take her for her walks. To do this, we would have to wear a bee-keeper's glove, because she would try to tear our hands & arms to shreds.

Now what?

Somebody rooting around in the kitchen again. What are my social obligations to my apartment-mates when they use the kitchen, which is right in front of my face as I lean here warbling, at 2:11 in the morning? I don't feel up to any conversation right now... I need a conversation with an Inspiration -

I feel like asking the *I Ching* some questions, but I can't think of any for which I could hope to understand the answers.

Maybe I should go to sleep, but why? What is my ideal, if I go to sleep now? I should go out & try to get laid. At 2:30? Maybe it's too late. Everyone is taken by now.

Am I hungry, or full? Have I eaten today? Oh yes - pancakes.

Phone - ring!

Radio - silence!

Man - sleep...

Love - approach!
Muffins - be of good corn!

Thurs. A.M. May 10. 3:15.

Who can sleep?

I hate this casual Jew-bating in Henry Miller. Here this Jew has evidently put him up, fed him, etc. - and all he does is put the Jew down. Fuck Henry Miller. About women all he tells you is how fat they are and how wet they are. He is a perfect example of that variety of writer whose reputation is largely a matter of self-proclamation, echoed by the lazy and growing with the fortunes of the lazy who echo it. Well, he became a big success... Norman Mailer is quoted on the cover of the book, saying "...Henry Miller is the greatest living American writer..." I wonder if William Burroughs can now sue Norman Mailer -

After all, didn't he say, on the cover of Burroughs' book - "The only living American writer who could conceivably be possessed of genius!"

Does Mailer mean to say that altho Burroughs is the only one possessed of genius, Miller is still the best? Does that mean the best living American writer isn't even a genius?

3:41.

Bad. This is the 3rd or 4th day/night of confused sleeping pattern. Why? Shld. go to sleep right now. Turn off the radio. Sony Trinitron is being advertised. "Trinitron at Intercounty in New Ultrecht, New York!"

The average American consumes 10,000 grams of sodium a day. We must fool the taste buds by using up to three times the herbs and spices you would normally use, so says the radio... People will rave about the taste, and no one will ask where is the salt shaker...

Back to the music. Harps and the soft voice of braggadocio worm forth from this little Japanese Idol, my radio.

I remember when I first saw that Grove Press Edition of *The Naked Lunch* in the Greenpoint Drug Store, across the street from Johns Hopkins, where I was a freshman - and it was just spring - the first time I had ever seen the spring in a semi-rural setting - and there it was, in red letters, "Only ... conceivable ... genius ..." and, wanting to be a writer myself I decided it was worth picking it up. And the fact is, he is very good, very funny, etc., and I took him gladly as a master, but now, after all the years of reading that dry stuff, benevolence disguised as malevolence, advice disguised as mimesis, you finally have to say - "There's got to be something better than this slightly Victorian, gout-y, tone of voice for everything."

Still, I had many happy years copying Burroughs, along with Beckett, and I will always be grateful...

But still, something *must* be on the way - It *must* be - I feel like the guy who said: "One is coming after me and I'm not even fit to tie His shoelaces..."

I look for him. The English language looks for him. You can feel the words are just lining up for him - they're getting into position for the next big dance ... when the master user comes... Will he be blind? Who knows. Will he be blind?

4:23 A.M.

"Crazy Eddie, the man who drove you crazy at home, now wants to drive you crazy in your car! Crazy Eddie! His prices are *in*-sane!"

"Only a few days till Mother's Day at Markell Jewelry, the place to *buy* your gold and *sil*ver, and *sell* your *di*-monds, darlin'! Get Mom a *watch* at Markell Jewelry, the place with gold *bands*, silver *bands*, di-mond *bands* - she'll love you every time she checks out that jewelled *face*, darlin'!"

(Now, a song:)

"Them young girls they after *you*, girls! - They all over you like *white* over rice!"

"Show me a bankbook with a whole *lot* of zeroes after the first five numbers!"

"Show me some blue chips and I don't mean food stamps, honey..."

May 10. 5:13 A.M.

Pull back the batik to get the dawn breezes... Why does the wind act up at dawn and dusk?... Look out at the courtyard. Listen to the pastel of the generators - or shld we say: water-color-sound of the generators? Look for the white cat, the tortoise cat... Usually they are on that fire escape, keeping guard over the architectural ruins of the courtyard. Downstairs lives an architect - I can tell by his mail - and he is the proprietor of the courtyard's ground surface, although for all I know he controls the air space too - anyway, he has foregone the traditional courtyard modes - There is no grass, no flower, no shrub, no hammock, no lawn furniture nor no bar-b-que. Instead we have irregular paving on which stand every conceivable kind of marble and stone column, and many eaves, and other decorative sculpted pieces off old buildings. Pompeii in a yard the size of four ping-pong tables, for the general delectation and improvement of all whose windows open over this collection of columns. However, I have yet to see him out wandering among the evocative shadows of his ruins, beneath either the moon or the sun. This might be because a complete session of wandering down there can be done in less than a minute, and would therefore be easy to miss unless I knew exactly when to look out... Now what? Sleep, or go out & get coffee and a corn muffin? Each has something to be said for it. It is 5:34 A.M. The sky is perfect, in that there is enough light to see by but not enough to read by, in that there is enough light to see by, but its source is not yet visible, and in that it is cool to the touch. I think I *will* go out, and then go to sleep later, after breakfast, and sleep while it's hot.

Sleep, tired brains; say "yummy, yummy," and go to corrupt meetings.

Thurs. May 10. 2:55 P.M.

I did sleep.

I slept from 5 AM to 1:55 PM. Marty and Joyce were on the way out when I awoke. He said "It's a great day for summer daytime sleeping." She's from Cyprus. Marty spent five years there and they were married there. Theirs is a great love story... He was a poet - now he runs a store in Soho selling things from Cyprus & North Africa. He was sitting on a hillside and he saw a beautiful girl go by on a bicycle. He followed her, but lost her in the rush-hour crowd. Then he waited at that time of day in the same spot for 3 months each day, until he saw her again. This time he was with a friend of his. They lost the girl again, but the friend knew her family. Marty finally arranged to be allowed to visit Joyce's family. In Cyprus, when courting a girl, you meet with the family a few times before they let you talk to the girl. He said immediately he wanted to marry their daughter. They were offended & her mother threw him out. Then he had to give some money to some of the relatives, so they would plead his case with the mother that he be allowed to visit once again. He finally got back into the house and after several months of courting the entire family, he married Joyce. Now they are both here, amazed at how few New Yorkers have ever *heard* of Cyprus, let alone know anything about it - considering the historic importance and current troubles of the island. I said, "Polls show 10% of the nation has never heard of the President of the U.S."

How can Marty wear a blazer and a wool sweater in this heat?

I'm glad I slept. I feel less like I'm about to blast off than I have in 72 hours...

Then I went out to the Coffee Time Coffee Shoppe for two cups of coffee and a corn muffin the size of my hat... Down to the Idle Hour Books and Magazines to look at the latest slick pornography as well as the less eternal journals filled with many opinions about all that which is about to kill us.

One of the magazines has an exclusive bunch of photos, evidently taken thru a telescopic lens, of Caroline, Princess of Monaco, daughter of Grace Kelly, naked on a yacht somewhere off the coast of France. Now that I think of it, why didn't I get that magazine? There is certainly nothing I'd rather be looking at. Definitely not that work-shirted, myopic woman on the opposing fire escape babbling to her plants.

Now, I won't go out until dark. Fuck this sunlight. The secret of weather is, that when it is cold, the sun should be bright - when it is warm, the sun should be covered. However, the cruelty of climate is such that these perfect unions are the most rare.

Now, Joyce has just come downstairs with her hair in rollers. She is going to be in a fashion show up on 59th street, at the Coliseum. The show is sponsored by the Cypriot Government. Joyce will wear the costume of a princess, all gold. She comes from a land that has spirits for each locality, for each tree, each road, hill, house, stone, year, month, day, family... Now, she is having a few chicken heads, left over from dinner, along with some duck's feet, to give her strength to wear that headdress.

Thurs. May 10. 3:48 P.M.

I looked out the window of the front room. The people in the street are walking as though blasted from exploding grenades and staggering toward enemy lines.

Suicide is a strange way to go. Although, why think of that?

Suicide is a perfect example of an action taken at a time when no action was called for.

I remember now what I was peripherally thinking of - the source of this suicide - considering:

I was in the University Bar two nights ago and I saw that guy I've seen every time I've gone into the bar.

The thing about this guy is that he looks a lot like someone who used to go to college with me, whose name was Stanley. So much so that I thought it *was* Stanley.

Now the thing about Stanley is, that although I didn't really know him when we were at school, I believe he is in possession of the answer to a mystery which has been mysterious to me for many years now.

For Stanley was the best friend of another boy, named Steve. They played in the same band. They were part of a very hip group of people, I remember, at least by our limited lights, at school. I didn't know Stanley very well, and I didn't know Steven very well.

About two years after I got out of college I went back to Baltimore to visit my friend Jack. At the time, Jack lived in a one-room windowless apartment under the stairs in an old bldg. on St. Paul St.

I was there alone, in bed. It was about 3 in the afternoon. The door opened and in walked somebody. The room was totally black, even to my eyes, which had been used to it for about an hour, so the one who entered could not see me there. I was about to say, "Jack?" thinking it must be, when the one who had entered started talking, rapidly, without greeting the one to whom he thought he was speaking. He said, "Alright, Jack, I'm going to kill Michael. Did you hear me?"

I said: "Mmm."

He said: "I have that gun you sold me, and I have bullets - I thought he'd be here today, that's why I came. I heard he was in town. Pam said she saw him with you in the Blue Jay. Do you know where he is now?"

Hearing this, I recognized the voice as Steven's, and for the first time I understood that what I had thought up to that moment, was a joke, was no joke. Jack had said, the night before, that Steven was looking for me to kill me, but he was laughing when he said it, and there was no reason I knew of - or know of to this day - for Steven to hate me, or feel anything for me one way or the other.

I cleared my throat and tried to sound as though he had awakened me (or rather, Jack) from a deep sleep. "Uh-Uh, - Err" I said from under the covers.

"Oh, I'm *sorry*, man! Shit, I'm *really* sorry! I didn't know you were asleep!" he said, suddenly hyper-polite and obviously feeling he'd been presumptuous. He said, "I'll just go look around the campus for him, man, maybe he went over there. Sorry, man!" and he trod tall-ly out the door.

As for me, as I say, I was not totally taken by surprise to hear what Steven had said. Only because Jack and his brother Phillip had both laughingly told me when I got to town that Steven *was* looking for me, to kill me. When I had been doubtful, and said, "Where would he get a gun?" that was the biggest joke of all, and Phillip - a young man of unusually daredevilish habits - laughed so hard he fell off his chair and banged his head against the wall. The reason it was so funny was that Jack was the one who had sold Steven the gun.

"Well," said Jack, sensitively nodding his long femur bone and staring into a cup of steaming tea, "he didn't tell me what he wanted it for until *after* I sold it to him. And anyway, he paid me 50 dollars." It was a .38 Police Special.

Jack said: "One quite unlooked-for aspect in all this is the fact that Steven is reportedly spending his time drilling holes in the bullets and cutting the heads with a razor blade." "What does that mean" I asked, thinking it might be a religious function.

"Well, it means the bullet spreads out when it makes contact with its target, so where you might have had - oh - a 50 centimeter exit wound now you have the capability, at least, of blowing away the entire back, or head, of your victim."

"Fabulous," said I.

Thus, I knew what Steve was talking about when he said he was going to kill me, but I didn't know *why*.

Why?

This is the mystery, to me.

When I asked Jack, he said he had never been clear on that. Of course, it had to do with the fact that Steven - who was ahead of his time in many things - was also one of the first people to take the drug Angel Dust - and after a couple of years he had lost his senses under its influence. The only thing Steve ever said *against* me, according to Jack, was that he had come over to my place one night and had wanted to talk to me, but that while he was talking I fell asleep.

"But he understood that!" I protested - "I apologized when he came over! He was speeding his ass off and I was tired! He knew that!"

Jack smiled and spread his hands. "I'm just telling you what *he* said."

"And that's *all* he said?"

"Well, you know, he wanted to be your friend, and he felt you rejected him."

"Because I fell asleep? I was *tired*!"

"Who can explain the mind of a madman?" asked Jack, who had sold this particular madman a Police Special.

"Did you sell him the bullets, too?" I asked.

He said, "What did I need the bullets for without the gun?"

So, soon after Steve had departed that dark room, I switched on the light, packed my suitcase, left a note for Jack and took a cab to the train station, where I got the first train back to New York.

That night, Jack called me in New York and told me that Steve had looked for me all over Baltimore during the day and that, failing to discover me, he had gone back to his own apartment and used the gun on himself, and had blown his head off his shoulders.

Since then, I have asked Jack, and I asked a girl I met out in California who was the wife of one of Steve's friends in those Baltimore days - why did he want to kill me? But no answer has come from any source.

And that is what I wanted to ask the guy in the University Bar, whom I've seen every time I've ever gone in there, and thought was Stanley. The reason I didn't ask him any of the other times I was in there, is that, as much I do want to know the answer, I do not want to know the answer. Still, two nights ago I decided, I must have courage, and ask Stanley. But when I went over to him, he wasn't Stanley. He had never been to Baltimore. He didn't even speak English. He was a Spanish NYU student.

Thurs. May 10. 6:43 P.M.

Marty and his wife are at the fashion show. *I Ching* tells me not to call Sammy. It says I better not waste my money on heroin. I'll be broke again very soon. It's definitely something to think about. I do like the much more civil manner in which everyone treats you when you have a little money. Still, it's a temptation... To feel peaceful! How difficult can that be? Why go all out for it? Why don't I let it creep over me? I do feel like calling Sammy. What will I do?

6:50. The News is on in 10 minutes. I'll watch that.

Friday. May 11. 12:14 A.M.

Have not called Sammy.

Instead, I strolled down 7th Avenue, into the Chez Stadium, for pork chops, broccoli and potatoes. And there read the *Times*, which informed me that the US and Russia have agreed on the disarmament treaty, that the Iranian Revolutionary Council has executed their first civilians - one was a man accused of feeding his enemies to the lions in the circus he owned; the other was a 69-year old Jewish millionaire, the "plastics king" of Iran, accused of "spying and raising money for Israel." The standard charge they use for everyone over there is, "crimes against God and His Emissaries, and being a friend to the enemies of God." They have some other original, hard phrases, like being "a corruptness on the earth."

The Revolutionary Council commandeered the property of the plastics king, while issuing a statement that the rights of religious minorities in Iran would be protected - "especially those with a Holy Book," they said. Still, the Ayatollah made a radio broadcast to the people of Egypt telling them to "chop off the hands of Anwar el Sadat" for making peace with Israel.

They have just returned from the fashion show. Marty tells me he met an editor from Collier Books who told him he has $3 million at his disposal to develop a new series of books. I would like to do these books of news photos with funny captions, or words coming out of the mouths of the people in the photos, and since I told the idea to Marty, he has referred to it exclusively as our joint project, so now we'll meet with this editor and try to get an advance. We should *do* a few of the captions, to show the editor. But will we? We have been discussing the book for eight months, as though it's some huge hurdle, the overleaping of which, if we can only get the energy to do it, will rescue us from the financial ruin that is constantly upon us, each in his own way... "Ah, when we do our photo captions, *then* we'll be able to take vacations, *then* we'll be able to pay the phone bill, etc...

I feel the need to write a book - is it a novel? Sniff sniff... Maybe... A book of short stories? Sniff sniff sniff... Maybe... Who cares what it is, just spin out that thread, in whatever form it takes - I really don't care - I'd like to write a three thousand foot span of words, all in an unknown genre. Like a liquid that would not fit into any known vase. Does such a thing exist. Why not? Murky passageways, biscuit-like circuitry traversing it throughout.

But who will need such liquid as that description postulates? Drinkers with unknown spaces of emptiness, which they must fill without naming the liquid to fill them, not the largest group within any population, but not the smallest... Are they having a party in this heat? Why don't some of those rock musicians take some of those high-voiced and deep-voiced girls out onto the fire escape and there, within my sight, take off their blouses? This is a dull night, and that music is not helping. Aren't you warm in that stuffy loft? Let's go!... Ah, but now we see *why* they have not come out on the fire escape - we see *why* we are hearing 90% male voices and only 10% female... Whenever their record player reaches an interstice between two songs, one is able to hear the actual conversation of the party, and it is uniformly concerned with one topic: record deals... the dollar potential of the celebrants... Just today I heard them practice their songs - very intellectual stuff - the melody is a march-beat to which they tell advice and issue warnings - New Wave ... Advice, complaints and versions of old songs like

"Town Without Pity." Just pay them and get them off this block.

Fri. May 11. 3:34 A.M.

Marty and I have just been trying to think of a way to retaliate against the musician or musicians who live across the courtyard. He is in favor of a bag filled with shit, to be launched through the gaping transoms, which are always open, proving the inhabitants need air... I wonder if Sammy is over there trying to sign the group for Buddha Records. Then, when all the junkies call him for their supplies over the next few weeks we will be regaled with their music on his answering machine. That is what he does, to honor his new groups. Think of what that will mean to me.

Went through Washington Square Park, after dinner. It's very weirdly attractive now that it has been redesigned for easier access by police cars. Everyone was smoking grass or exchanging pills for dollars, or something in barter on the West side of the circle. On the East side there was a black man holding the attention of about 200 people with his comedy routine. He said: "Most of this what I'm doing is improvisation. I'm making it up as I go along," and he got a huge hand for that, so I thought he must be pretty good. Soon after that a heckler spoke from the crowd. The comedian was improvising about the full moon, which he pointed toward, with its few clouds ringed around it, partially covering it. He said we would soon use up the Earth, and would all go to the Moon to work. He imitated a white man walking to work on the moon, with his typical walking motions amplified by the lack of gravity. He showed sex on the Moon, but it didn't make sense the way he did it. The heckler said: "Go on, Richard Pryor!" and he said: "My name is not Richard Pryor, it's Charlie Barnett; I live in Harlem and I have a summer home in fuckin' Newark." The crowd loved that. Then the heckler said: "Tell a lie, man! Hey man, tell a lie! So the comedian said: "Tell a lie? Alright - you're fuckin' normal, that's a lie." The comedian didn't have any shirt on. He was just a thin, bony man, not very tall, with his shirt wrapped around his waist, and his rhetoric had attracted all these people to hear what he had to say. He didn't insult white people so badly that they would leave in terror, but he did insult them badly enough so all would recognize the truth, or the piece of truth at the center of each proposition. He seemed to be proof of what my father told me about comedians - that their humor, although it seems to be based on insults, is actually based on compliments.

It started to rain and the crowd reluctantly dispersed, mostly forgetting to throw change for the performer. Charlie Barnett, however, stood his ground, like the captain of a ship, waiting to see that all his passengers had gotten to safety before thinking about himself even so much as to put his shirt on. Then he looked at the rainy sky which had dispersed his crowd, and said: "All right you fucker," as though he were putting down another heckler, and he walked off the visible spot down toward Bleecker Street.

Then I walked up University over to Fifth, over to Sixth, up to Fifteenth... the rain stopped before I got home. Can't sleep, can't sleep till daylight. Feel those delightful breezes... Bad weather in the wheat belt could send bread prices up 3%. The farmers can't plant the Spring wheat. Is that any excuse? We'll leave that to wiser heads to decide... What's this?

A flesh-colored spider!

Now where is it?

Is it crawling up the side of the mattress? No, there it is on the wall. Forget it. Don't think about it. They're very good to have around. The flesh colored ones are just children, anyway. Grow up to kill the flying ants.

Fri. May 11. 4:07 A.M.

Not this old western with Dana Andrews and Susan Hayward again! And who's the other guy - we'll see him soon - not exactly George Brent, but someone far more similar to George Brent than anyone else I can think of - What else is on? Tom & Jerry. I ought to watch this, the better to write my cartoon feature science fiction classic... Look - Jerry is having a dream... A dream-mouse comes and taps him on the sleeping shoulder ... leads him out of the mouse hole to a table with blueprints on it. I get it. The dream-mouse is a blue-print outline. Now Jerry and the Blueprint Mouse are running away from the Blueprint Cat. All without words. All very mathematical. One hypothecates the future historians who will wonder: how is it that for 50 years once in America, while all other genres swelled and died, while musicians starved and painters urinated on their canvases for want of anything more original to offset them from all the other painters with whom they were cheek by jowl, struggling for an income - *why* did this survive and grow year after year? The cat chasing the mouse, the coyote chasing the Road Runner - What arcane sanhedrin gathered the writers and artists to feed the world's insatiable craving for mice? MGM. "Made in Hollywood, U.S.A." I worked there. I wrote the dialog for a giant computer to say, before, during, and after the rape of the beautiful girl, played by Julie Christie. I have just figured out what was wrong with that picture! She should have been rescued *before* being raped! Who wants to see the heroine get raped, even if it is by a witty computer who fashions his own stainless steel dick down in the conveniently located basement laboratory. George Lucas would have caught that. That's what makes him so popular. And if she had been *saved*, we could have ended the film with the race against time, the cross-cutting between the rapidly-constructing penis in the lab, coming together out of tiny metal pyramids that somehow get into a flaming furnace, there to form themselves into a rough estimation of a dick, and the Hero - her husband who as it was, had his entire part cut and is left to come in at the end. If she had been *saved*, Fritz could have been shown: 1) figuring it out, 2) hopping in his jeep, 3) going through red lights, 4) running out of gas, 5) getting out & running the last ten blocks, 6) running up the pathway, 7) breaking down the door with his shoulder, 8) looking back and forth, 9) engaged in hand to hand combat with the one handed wheelchair which acted as the computer's henchman (the hand had been rented from Harvard University), and 10) having knocked out the wheelchair, 11) untied his wife from the table and beaten back the pyramidal dick with a Breuer chair...

Back to Dana Andrews and ... George Brent? Brett something? Brent something?... And here comes Hoagy Carmichael! "Sitting in the Saddle, I watch the Stars Skidaddle..." He is riding on a mule named Susie ... where is Lenny? He was supposed to call before now. I must eat. I'll call him...

He's out at Maisie's - He'll meet me at the Chariot in 30 minutes. I'll go now, and approach the Chariot in a wide circle, gathering newspapers on the way there.

Saturday. May 12. 5:02 A.M.

Took my sliver of orange biscuit to keep me happy until gentle sleep.

What have I been doing? Twelve hours ago ate salmon (individual can) salad, talked to Lenny about the writing game. Lenny used to be a poet, when I met him years ago in Berkeley, now he's off poetry and he writes articles for magazines. Usually, but not always, he does interviews. He has a small tape recorder he carries in a yellow slicker satchel. The magazines are incredibly cheap w/writers, when you think about it. Now he's writing a sex column for *High Times* and they pay $250 per column! This from a magazine that probably makes a half million dollars every month, from the advertising of drug paraphernalia. The manufacturers of hash pipes, grass sifters, coke spoons, pill bottles and rectal hash pipes, have no place to advertise their products except in *High Times*. But do the owners of it share that windfall? Here, Lenny has a wife, a baby. Makes the sensitive artist want to kill somebody. Magazine & newspaper writers ought to unionize. Think of the excess value each one generates by his labor - the money accruing to the publication because of the writer that exceeds the amount he is paid. The weather has gotten cooler. There were a lot of love scenes enacted on 6th avenue as we sat there. How great, these couples turning toward one another and embracing feverishly. What movie stars! This one girl I remember in particular, a redhead with a voluptuous body that looked as though she had just jumped into the air and was not yet completely settled back on earth -

She was kissing her boyfriend and rolling her hips in circles - then she'd look into his eyes with powerful force - What an orange dress! What high heels! What's the use! Then we went to the Exotic Ice Cream Store to watch Hockey Highlights. Lenny is a big Rangers fan. He said when he started following hockey, he felt like some kind of weirdo, that it was a weird, foreign sport, but now everyone follows it.

Cut to 12 midnight.

Lenny, having gone to Long Island City on the train, now returns in his car, accompanied by Maisie. Maisie is Lenny's wife's sister. She's good looking - very skinny - wearing white ankle socks - sat on my bed and we watched Johnny Carson. Richard Pryor was on, miraculously transfigured by a trip to Africa. Whereas he usually intimidates the host, now he is enthusiastically kissing Johnny's ass ... says he feels everything "in my heart..." That's the end of him... He says a few words about some white girl he went to Africa with.

Where did we go?

A party, where everyone kept saying "Are you a friend of Ramu?" The Mud Club, where Maisie got us in by whispering into the ear of the young lawyer they had guarding the door... How noble to be one of the ones let in... How dismal once inside, be you on the second or the first floor... Came home. Sammy called at 5 A.M. Said he'd been trying to reach me all day. His connection told him he better get his money together, because the stuff we like is running out. I told him I was ready right then, but he said the guy was asleep then. The guy is an accounting student at Bernard Baruch college of Business. He & his wife have a nice little heroin trade. The price is high, but the quality is good. They're the Zabar's of the junk world. Sam will call at around noon. It is now 6:39 A.M. It seems Maisie lives with a guy who plays bass for a group. I asked her if she ever cheated on him. She said five times in seven years. "Is he a stud?" "No." I gather he is younger than she. He loves science fiction. She said she has to hear everything he does behind her back. She's a fanatic for honesty.

6:46

5 hrs. and 14 minutes, (about), until Sam calls or I call him. I'm doing wrong. This is wrong. I know it, but what can I do? I don't have any motivation for anything else. I remember when I used to be motivated. But that was in the smokey past, not now; now I can't think of one single goal, except to get high. What went wrong? Nothing went wrong. I used to think about my next meal. This is a form of progress.

Lenny said Maisie always advises him to cheat on his wife, her sister, if that's what he really wants to do. She said, "I feel terrible - I mean it is my *own sister* - but I'm the one who has to hear his fantasies all the time."

"Yeah, Maisie tells me I should do it, but she never just says, 'Look, Lenny, come here in the back room with me,' I wonder why."

"Sisters!" says I, with a sigh.

"Sisters!" James Hayes says: "If you can get one sister, you can get all of them."

Maisie denied it.

All this took place over plates of fettucine alfredo and fried zucchini. What does it mean that we live in a time in which these two foods are served everywhere? I drank three cups of coffee, while Maisie looked around for women who were crazy about Lenny and pointed them out to me.

Sunday. May 13. 5:35 A.M.

This just took place at the tavern owned by Lou Belicosi star of *Night Lines*... Self and two friends (unfortunate enough to have entered with me) personally ejected by Belicosi. Was it a lesson?

There was rain. It was gray. I woke at 4 in the afternoon. Lenny called & asked about the show. Could we get in? Frank, the producer of the show, is a friend of mine. I have gone before, and have told Lenny how much fun it was. Also, Lenny has been trying to get an interview with Belicosi for 2 months now, and he has not been having any luck getting to the very Famous, Great, guy... Lenny said he needed Belicosi. He has an idea for an article he can sell to *Oui* Magazine, called "Loafing," but *Oui* won't buy unless he includes Celebrities among those asked how they loaf. Actually, they'd rather have celebrities only, although Lenny has been trying to convince them it is the quality of any given tale of loafing that will make or break it, not the fame of the loafer. Still, names they want, names you have to give them. Knowing this, I realized I must call Frank and ask to go to the show. Also, Maisie wanted to go, and I thought it would be nice to see her. Therefore, I did call. By the time I reached him it was 10:30, an hour before the show, so there were no more tickets. However, he said we could come and stand with him on the floor of the studio, and watch him as he produced the show.

After the show Tom James, who had sung on the show, found out I had some dope, and he asked me for some. We went into a corner office and I opened the envelope and gave him some. He had sung a song about a mill worker, and I said I had liked the song very much, and that it had reminded me of two girls I met once up in Maine, who worked in a shoe factory. One of them had to reach into a glue pot all day to glue the tops of the shoes to the soles, and she had said every one who had her job got cancer from the glue. He said that was the kind of factory the song was about, and that the industrial revolution came to that region of the country first, so the factories there are often the oldest, most hazardous, most unhealthy, of all... I put some dope on a memo pad, and he said: "I think you should realize I have a very high tolerance for that stuff." I should have just said, "Right" but I said, "I think you should realize I have a very low tolerance for giving it away." It was a joke, but still - Pride. After all, did I begrudge a poet this respite from life, especially when he had been working? No, I just had to open my big mouth. I should have given more to him. I should not have tried to be smart. I should have openly shown my appreciation for his poetry. I now believe the thing that happened later was the judgment upon me - for my act of pride when I gave that gift, not graciously enough, to that poet... After leaving the T.V. station, went to a restaurant on 81st street, and then down to Belicosi's private club, on a deserted street in lower Manhattan.

Sunday. May 13. 5:08 P.M.

No, on second thought ... let me just shave, watch some T.V. ... there's Nadia Comanicci the Roumanian gymnastic champion ... what a serious, one might say, "tough" girl!... Hark! The phone:

"I don't want to..."

"Well, all right, come over then."

"What am I doing? I'm writing in a notebook."

"Yes, even as we speak."

"Yes, that's why I hesitated. Usually, as you know I'd jump at the chance... But I'm writing something... No idea ... could be, could be, but who knows? I'm not naming it yet ... come over, I'll tell you about how Lou Belicosi threw me out of his club last night. You can make me dinner... Goodbye... Yes, I have some but you can't have any!... Well, OK, but that's all, I *need* it, you're a dilettante... Of course I need it, not for fun, to work on... Goodbye..."

That was Robin. Did you see how I kept my emotional distance? I've learned from long experience with Robin that the moment she senses you need her, she takes that opportunity to transform herself into a cruel bitch.

Monday. May 14. 11:17 A.M.

No sleep last night.

First, let me finish what I started, about pride...

We get down to the bar owned by Belicosi. A doorman & Belicosi's co-star let us in, then Belicosi grabs me by the arm and says "What are you doing here?" I thought he must be kidding, for he must have heard me when I had told both doorman and co-star that Frank had invited me down there. Thinking Belicosi was making some kind of joke, I said, "Oh, I thought this was the Kit-Kat Klub. I'm with the tour bus," or something like that. B. did not laugh. Instead, he said, "OK! He's out! He's out! Get him out of here!" I smiled. I was sure now he *was* joking, so I smiled and said "Heh heh" to indicate that I understood. However, since he was not joking, my indication only fuelled his anger. I went to the bar and got a beer. I was talking to some friends near the bar. Belicosi passed by and said, "I'm sorry man but you really have to get out of here. Like now man." Then he walked away, and *again* I thought: What a kidder! Although by now I was beginning to question Belicosi's famous sense of humor. It was easy to have respect for the straight face he was keeping, but was that enough to warrant this beating of a dead horse? Lenny said softly, "Are you sure he's kidding?" I said, "Yes." Then B. came back and said, "Please, please, I don't want to have to tell you again, this is a private club and I don't know you and I'd like you to please leave!" I said, "You mean you're serious! I thought you were kidding!"

He shook his head, looked at the floor, then looked up at me from beneath his thick black brows. "Come on, now, I'm trying to tell you." he said.

"All right," I said, "Sure, I mean, I'll leave, but is there any particular reason?"

He said, "Yes, there is, man."

I said, "Is is because I said, 'Is this the Kit Kat Club?'"

"That's part of it," he said, "you were being a wise-ass, and we don't have wise-asses here."

I suddenly remembered the only reason I was out at all, was that Lenny had wanted to get an interview with none other than the very Belicosi I now seemed to have offended, and I tried to assure Belicosi that no offense had been meant.

I forgot to say that earlier, after my immortal line, "Isn't this the Kit Kat Club?" Belicosi had said, "All right, you want to take this outside? Let's go outside!" and his co-star had said, "You better take off your jacket, friend," to me, "He really wants to fight you." Then Belicosi had gone outside and stood between two uniformed chauffeurs he seemed to know, talking to them. I had followed him out with a grin on my face, but when he didn't look in my direction I thought, "I guess I fell for it," and went back inside.

I said, "You know, I don't crash parties. I'm only here because I was invited." He said, "What can I tell you, this isn't Frank's place, this is my place, it isn't his place." He stood looking at me a while, then started looking around the dark room. He said, "Did he come with you?"

"Who?"

He pointed to some guy far away, a tall figure.

"No."

"Did he come with you?"

He pointed to a man leaning against the bar wearing a cowboy hat.

"No, he didn't come with me."

"Well, whoever came with you has to leave. I'm sorry. Collect every one you came in with and leave. I don't know what else to tell you..." It was beginning to sound as though his lawyer was the cause of this order that I be evicted, and not himself.

I said, "I'm going. I'm on my way, but I have to wait for a girl I came with." Maisie was on the phone. When she returned we left. Before that, Lenny leaned down to speak into Belicosi's ear, saying: "Now that this is the worst possible moment, do you think this is a good time to ask you to give me an interview?"

Belicosi shook his head. He folded his arms over his chest. When Maisie got back we told her we had gotten thrown out. She said to Belicosi: "I'm sorry I ruined your party," and the three of us left. I said: "Anyone can get *in* to that place. It takes a great talent to get thrown out." Then came the slightly embarrassing job of explaining to Maisie what had happened, and telling Marty the next day. Marty said Belicosi was looking for someone to beat him up. That was why he had challenged me to a fight. He said, "You should have followed him outside and given him a real *shot*, one of those real shots, that would have doubled him over, and you would have been on page six of the Post today."

I said, "I never thought of hitting him."

My own theory is that the Universe had decided to teach me a lesson. I *had* been a wise-ass to Tom James, the singer, and had not suffered then. Thus, the Universe was saying to me: "You didn't show respect to one artist - the poet - we paid you back through another artist - the comedian."

For it was as though Belicosi were punishing me for the words I had said to Tom James, as though he were the tracking hound of the muses, and had caught me several blocks away from the scene of my crime.

Afternoon.

In the same way, a general period of retribution seems to have started as soon as I broke up with Susan. With the Universe paying me back quite honorably, and understandably for my crimes against her, and against our love.

A certain New Year's Eve was the dividing line. About which, the less said the better.

After that, we separated. I went to New Haven to finish a book about Algeria. I had started out to write a very gung-ho book about Algeria, but I didn't like it there. I tried to escape the necessity of having to say I didn't like it, by totally evading the true story of our experience, Susan's and mine, Algeria, and instead inventing the story of a young cyclops I claimed we met running around on the streets of old Algiers. I told the story of our daily meetings and conversations with this cyclops child - whose name was Aqbal for some reason I now forget - as though it were all true and he was a real child, twelve years old. I even created photographs of little Aqbal, by covering the two eyes of a school child whom Susan had photographed, replacing them with one single eye, directly above the nose. I had photos of Aqbal attending an outdoor class, with the old teacher sitting on the cobblestones, writing on a blackboard held upright by another student; Aqbal coming out of a soccer game, with all the elated fans around him; Aqbal and myself talking seriously to a minister of the National Bank, and so on. As far as I could tell, the cyclops child was clearly presented as a fictional character, but when I went in to the publishing company to talk to the editor of the book one time, she said something about how it would sell a million copies if we could just get Aqbal over here, and put him on the Johnny Carson Show. Possibly because of my recent break-up with Susan, I wasn't as alert as I might otherwise have been, to the dangers inherent in the situation, and I made the foolish mistake of smiling crookedly and saying, "Huh?"

The woman said, "I mean, do you think his parents would let him travel? We'd pay all expenses, of course for Aqbal and both of his parents, if they want to come with him. His father seems like quite a character from the way you describe him. Slaughtering that sheep in his white yachting pants like that and everything. Wow."

I said, "I mean, Aqbal's a fictional character. I'm glad he comes across like he's real but he really isn't."

That was a mistake. It ended, so soon after the period of grace in my love life had ended, the period of grace in my work life.

The woman looked confused for a brief flicker, then said, "Well, I don't understand. If the cyclops isn't real, what are these photographs? Why the long descriptions of your testing him for e.s.p.? Why all that stuff about scientists trying to study poor Aqbal in their labs? The whole thing is nothing but a hodge-podge, if it isn't true. It's meaningless. And we extended your advance payments twice. Where's the book we contracted for? A figment of your imagination can't go on the Johnny Carson show." The company sued me for the return of the advance.

That kind of thing never would have happened to me when I was with Susan.

That was 8 yrs. ago.

The last time I saw Susan was February last year. Seventeen months ago.

At that time we were very quiet together, as though someone had died in the next room. Nothing clicked. She looked great, she said she was about to graduate from an art course, she wouldn't talk about her boyfriends or any adjacent topic.

Then, a year after that I was in L.A. and I got a call from her, from back East. She said, "You'll never guess what. I'm getting married."

I said, "Why?"

"It's funny," she said, and I heard her inhaling her cigarette, "last night I dreamed I called you and told you this, and you said: 'Why?' exactly as you just did."

"What did you dream would be your answer?"

"It seems like this is the right thing for me to do right now."

"Does it? Good. Congratulations. That's great. Who is it, anyone I know?"

"Well, I think you may have met him a few years ago. His name is Ben. He lives here in Provincetown."

"All year around?"

"Mm-hmm."

"Sounds depressing."

"Well - he edits a magazine here so he has to be here."

"Is that what he does?"

"Well, partly. He's a poet."

"A poet, that's great. They're terrific, poets."

"Mm. But it's funny. You know, he wants me to sign a pre-nuptial agreement."

"You're kidding. What is he, afraid you're going to take 50 percent of his poems if you get a divorce. A, B, A, B - You get the B's."

"Well, no, it's the magazine. He wants to be sure that's his. I think it's understandable."

I knew the implication of these remarks was that he had money, but I didn't say anything about it.

"I think it's weird. You love this person? How long have you known him?"

"Two weeks. He wanted me to live with him, but I said I never wanted to do *that* again - " (a bitter reminder of our past) " - so he said, 'Well, let's get married.' At first I thought it was crazy, but then I realized it was perfect."

"I mean, that's what you want?"

"Mm-hmm." puff puff puff

"What's the best thing about it?"

"Well, I'll be my own person. I mean, he gives me room."

"That seems like a better reason to be divorced, than married."

"Oh, now."

"Why don't you just have a nice pre-nuptial contract with him and marry me? I mean whatever I have, you can have lock, stock and barrel."

She laughed.

I said, "Evidently, you don't believe you and I are destined to be together again."

"That would be hard when we haven't been together for five years."

"Are you planning on having kids?" I asked, for some unknown reason.

"What!" she said, in total shock. "Uh-uh. No, not for a while, not yet."

"Why not?"

"I don't think I'm ready for that."

"How did you meet him?"

"It was when Andrew died. Everyone up here felt so badly, we all used to sit around crying, and he was a friend of Andrew's too, so I got to know him then." Andrew was a friend of ours, who died in his apartment after somehow cutting himself, while on angel dust. "You'd really like him," she said, "he's very intelligent. He had a mind like yours."

"Too bad for him. You know, I hope he's a good poet, because most of them aren't, and the ones that aren't, I think when they realize that, if they haven't given it up by then, it can tend to destroy their personalities. Are you afraid something like that might happen?"

She laughed at that one.

The funny thing was, after this conversation, until her marriage itself, it seemed we were more in touch, either on the phone or via letters, than we had been up to that time, for the past four or five years. Often I would tell myself to speak out, or to go back East to claim her for my own. My father, who has always loved her also, suggested, independently, I do just that, but for some reason I didn't act. I didn't move. In part, I felt mired down by my junk habit. I knew if I went back East, I would have to include a supply of junk among my belongings, and that at some point or other, whatever else was going on, I would have to retreat secretly to kick my habit, then to re-emerge as the worthy suitor my beautiful Susan deserved.

So she married another man. From her honeymoon, she sent me one last long letter I was very surprised to receive. As in other of her letters, there were many places where she *seemed* to say she still loved me, but nowhere was it clear, nowhere did it face me honestly from the page. It was always buried away.

Yes, and the length of those letters...

Anyway ... since then I have noticed life is receding from my immediate world. Where there used to be flowers, plants, cats & dogs, a woman, and me, all alive, just like on T.V., now there is only me, surrounded by paper, in many crooked stacks. Notebooks, pads, loose pages, index cards, magazines, both impure and pure, books, typed manuscripts, scrawled manuscripts, and in that corner we have the complete collection of newspapers and phone books, of our great city, and we can see the newspapers are curling their lips at me, halfway up to the mantelpiece. And of course we have the various cigarettes, rolling papers, ashes, more ashes, matches, paper plates I eat off of, paper cups I drink from, photos thumbtacked to the walls (all my friends are on one wall, and we're all watching Jesus, xeroxed over there on the opposite wall - the calm face on the Shroud of Turin) and of course the stacks of old letters, and of course...

Cough, cough ... cough ... cough, cough, cough...

Susan...

Cough ... cough, cough ... I smoke. I cough. I gag. I rest. I smoke. Yes, I have decided I am definitely in Purgatory...

I sinned against everything in sinning against the woman who loved me. That's the cheap crime. That's the crime every beginner commits, because, lo! it has no jail sentence!

Now, my punishment is to live in a world of paper ... Castles, spires, towers of paper, make the city wherein I cough.

You have to pay
No time off
Twenty-seven years

With the Same
cough...

I feel like Poe, and my wife is dead. I dwell among ruins. The floor of the sea awaits my step, the waves await my hat.

Tuesday. May 15. 4:36 A.M.

Fifty-eight degrees. Partly cloudy, clearing.

I slept from eleven in the morning to eight-thirty at night. Then I watched the news & *The Rockford Files*.

Ate breakfast at 3 A.M.

Sammy is being difficult again. James & I have been trying to score all day. Sam tells you how boring it is for him to go & score, how he isn't making anything out of it, how the guy he scores from is always sleeping, or away at Baruch Business College, or any number of other things. James calls him "The Blushing Virgin" because of his perennial reluctance.

The Blushing Virgin has a friend whom I have often seen over there. Last week I waited with this other friend - Teddy - while Sammy went to the East Side to get the stuff. Teddy & I got to talking and it turns out Teddy supplies Sam with most of Sam's stuff. Teddy said he'd call me the next time he got anything, thereby eliminating the middle man. Teddy has a deep suntan from a sunlamp. James knew at once who I meant when I said I had seen him there.

"Oh, yes, he's always there when you go over, with his eyes incredibly pinned. You know he brought the stuff, but they always try to make you believe he has nothing to do with junk, he's just a visiting photographer. Blushing Virgin and Photographer."

This is a very strange dawn here at 5:16, where it looks as though the day will be darker than the night was.

Marty saw "Manhattan":

"How can you make a movie about New York and not show one pan-handler, one bum, one rat? There were no black people in the whole movie except as chauffeurs and bellboys. I mean, *come on!* I mean, we can't do better than *that?* What is this? He's playing it safe, Woody Allen. They say he's moving away from the boffo comedy, he's moving away from the boffo comedy, but what is he moving towards? That's the question."

"You mean, it isn't great?"

"Not at all. It's that same old upper East Side neurotic bullshit. He plays the fuddy duddy, confused, bumbling... But you *know* what's behind it! It's like any man who doesn't take responsibility for his own life; his own actions. It's a pose. And as an homage to New York - Here he put his tongue out and ejected air around it. "All he shows is museums, Soho, a couple of bridges, so what? Sure, that Gordon Willis is a fucking genius... I'd like to have him in my corner, too. How can you go wrong? You just let him do his job, but that's not the director, that's the camera man..."

Marty shook his head. "I'm telling you, I could make a better fuckin' movie than that, and I'm going to get a cameraman, and *do* it! He didn't show 42nd street, 14th street - nothing - it's a shirking of responsibility. All right, so you can film scenes, you can show how people act & talk, great, but if you do it over & over, and you're supposed to be an artist, addressing your audience, the whole idea is, you're supposed to *try* at least, to make sense out of things, to draw a moral, to present an image of a *positive way to be* - present an image people can get some hope from..." He said, however, it was worth seeing for the photography and Mariel Hemingway.

Why do the breezes always start up at dawn and dusk? It's life energy, singing like the birds in the trees. Or rather, the same Life Energy that propels the dawn breezes, and the dusk breezes, propels the singing of the birds at those times... Trees in full bloom before fresh-sanded brick building and new-painted black fire escape... Billie Holiday on the radio - followed by - "God Bless the Child That's Got His Own."

NY Times. May 15, 1979.

About our neighborhood --

"Chelsea Persists as Ethnic Family Patterns Fade."

"Chelsea is not for families anymore, it's for individuals." said Helen Gilson, whose steel-blue Irish eyes reflect anger as well as resignation over the changes she has seen in 60 years.

"When you're born and raised in an area," she pointed out, "you want to stay there. But the city and real-estate people

forgot about the children in all the new housing, and now the kids can't afford to stay here."

The delicate ethnic fabric of Chelsea - the neighborhood between 14th and 34th Streets from the Avenue of the Americas to the Hudson River - has been shredded by slum-clearance programs that have forced out large numbers of families with Irish, Greek, Cuban, Spanish and Austrian heritage in the last 20 years.

"The real-estate ads play up Chelsea's multicultural aspect to attract new tenants, but in trying to cash in on the charm of the neighborhood, they're working to destroy it," said Amedeo Richardson, a writer who is working to maintain low-income housing in the area. "Chelsea is now a target for luxury exclusiveness and it makes me feel very sad and insecure about the future here."

This article fails to mention the Cuban-Chinese restaurants on Eighth Avenue. Ate at Asia de Cuba two nights ago.

7:36 A.M.

Fidel Castro returns to Mexico after 20 years. He left to start the revolution in Cuba, starting off from the Mexican Coast with 81 men, in 1956... Interest rates in for a long, steep climb... Gasohol fuelling a buying spree on Wall Street... Portrait of the Mellen Family: the Mellen Family is succeeding at staying wealthy... You can pick and choose from these quality White Rose Products, just like your Grandmother did... You give us 22 minutes, we'll give you the World... Taxi inspectors have stripped the medallions from 16 cabs... The Yankees lost, the Rangers are at Montreal... Borrow up to $10,000 with up to 10 years to pay... Modernize, new furniture, drapes, upholstery, and life-insurance is included at no extra charge... We're an equal housing lender...

A publication called "The Fiscal Observer" is going out of business. It is bankrupt.

Tues. May 15. 9:54 A.M.

Maisie called last night. She spoke very fast, as though she were speaking into a secret microphone. "This is Maisie. I got the name of that lawyer for your friend in California." She told me the name, and certain instructions concerning what to say to whom. I accepted it all as though it was the information I had been waiting most anxiously to learn. Actually, only later did I remember who was in need of a lawyer. I thanked her profusely. I said I'd tell my friend immediately. Then she invited me to see her boyfriend's band perform next Friday night at CBGB's. She said my name would be on the list. "That's great!" said I. I tried not to let on I had been asleep when she called; she was kind enough not to ask if I had been sleeping. I hope she didn't realize. You don't want people to know you sleep at all, let alone to know you sleep early in the evening.

End of Book I.

Book II

Tues. May 15. 9:12 P.M.

Time approximate. Am not with my digital clock. I am at Sam's, waiting for him to get back from the home of the connection, (or, man, as they used to say). He tells me the connection is a rich kid from Scarsdale. His father is a big rabbi. He's one member of a group of wealthy Jewish kids who have decided to live the "adventurous life of criminality." More to the point, he is the slowest drug dealer in the world! You always know Sammy will be at least an hour getting back, although all he has to do is give the rabbi's son our money and get the meager allotment, all wrapped in the little paper envelopes, each with its brand name and picture of a skeleton key, stamped in red ink.

Got here at 6:30, prepared for the usual one-hour wait. I had taken the precaution of asking Sam if he would be going right over there, or would he be stopping off at a disco, concert, rehearsal, or taping, or a press party. When I got here, he said the rabbi's son had just called, and said he would be out for about an hour - he had to get something downtown. Sam & I went out for dinner to kill the time. The evening was a little warm, a little cool. The streets of the West Side were filled with good-looking, young, straight-toothed, clean-haired, pressed-shirted or pressed-panted, girls and boys. I feel like an idiot spending money on dope. I haven't bought any clothing in 2 years.

Wednesday. May 16. 2:49 A.M.

After Sammy got back I apologized to him for having lost my temper earlier. When we got back from the restaurant, he was making calls, rolling himself a few joints, dragging around listlessly, though he knew I was waiting for him to go to the home of the connect. I finally shouted at him: "Come on, Sammy, do you have to stretch this out to every conceivable, never-ending, boring possible moment! Get *go*ing! Do it if you're going to do it!" Far from causing him to leap out the door, this unfortunate lapse on my part - after all, I had been very patient during dinner - knowing how Sammy places friendship above all else, how he does assert he never has made a dollar out of the thousands he has taken from me to exchange with his various connections for dope - now he had to sit down on the couch and say, "No, I don't stretch out the time, but your perception of me in that way bothers me, and I think we have to do something about that..." He finally went. When he got back, I said, "Look, I don't understand why you *don't* take a cut, or 10 dollars or 5 dollars from each sale - that only makes sense - "

He said, "I've been waiting for you to offer me some."

That put me on the spot. I gave him some, but from the package I had bought for Morris & Frank. Sammy and I went to Harrah's, where we saw "The Corruptions" with James White. Music very nice, anti-melodic, loud, James White good at heckling audience, looking like a handsome star, etc. good spitting.

The *I Ching* says it's OK to take junk, because I need the energy for something important that I do not yet have a glimmer of, either it or its nature, and that will somehow reverse the effects of my extravagance, or at least justify them.

We should understand, however, that my readings of the *I Ching* have a good chance of being mistaken. Still, I go on with this...

These gross and fine dependencies of mine.

3:18 A.M.

That's right! I have just recalled that girl, Cinderella, who first introduced me to the granular world of heroin. Three years ago - She cooked it in a brass dish, suspended over a thick white candle, like a small altar from which streams of smoke rose in "8"-shaped patterns... Cinderella, a small-eyed songwriter, quickly blew out the candle, threw a tiny white clump of something into the dish, and then picked up, from an old leather medical bag, an ancient-looking glass hypodermic syringe. She had a whole collection of these glass syringes, and long gleaming silver needles laid out on a white towel, drying. She carefully stuck the one in her hands into the dish, at an angle.

She filled the needle and wrapped a tourniquet around her upper arm, and now she pumped her fist, and flexed her arm, and flicked her finger against the inside of her elbow, all to cause one of her veins there to rise up sufficiently so that she could see it and plunge the needle into it. Finally, one such vein appeared, and she duly jabbed it, missed, then jabbed it again, until she thought she had the needle in there. She tested this proposition, in a manner I was to witness many times starting with that first time, by pulling back on the plunger and drawing her blood into the syringe, where it swirled around and mixed with the clear liquid already in there. Then, satisfied that she was in the vein, she pushed almost all the way down on the plunger, sinking the mass of liquid beneath the walls of her flesh, and sending it through her blood stream. The effect of the plunging action was instantaneous. Her eyes rolled back in her head, all the musculature of her back and neck seemed to turn to olive oil, so that she was sliding around through stages of further and further relaxation, and she said, "Aahh." Then she smacked her lips, gained control over her muscles again, and returned her attention to the needle and syringe still dangling from the crook of her arm. Instead of removing it, now that it had done its job, she once again pulled back on the plunger, *filling* once again the glass tube with the mixture of her blood and the dope, which she had been careful not to finish off in the first plunge. Then, after gazing at this dark red, almost black mixture, with an unmistakable look of satisfaction on her face, she again injected it into herself, this time all the way.

She then quickly removed the tourniquet from her arm, and after that, using a wad of cotton taken off the top of a bottle of clear alcohol, she pressed down on the spot of the injection, and removed the needle. Now for the first time, she looked at me, briefly.

She said, "Now you..." and without waiting for me to say anything, or even bothering to have her eyes lock onto the visionary track of my own, she turned to her envelopes and liquids, and tapped out a granular dash or two of white powder into the dish over the candle. Then she took up the clean needle, and used it to take water from a clean glass and squirt it into the brass dish. She lit the candle, and poked around at the cotton in the dish, tenderly, until the liquid started to boil. Then she put out the candle with her fingers, and went through the whole routine, I had seen a moment before.

I was ready. I was just past thirty, and feeling very tired of work, of struggle, effort, and all the frustrations of trying to earn a living as a writer in L.A., doing things I never set out to do, and that seemed (as they still do today) likely to occupy my life profitlessly and tediously, until the end thereof ... I wanted to do something that might release me from the daily pattern.

She wrapped the scarf around my upper arm, to cut off the flow of blood. She was humming, as she prepared the vein in my arm, and then shot the stuff into me. I was unable to watch for the first few times.

I stayed with her for two months, getting high every night and going to sleep just after Johnnie Carson's monolog, with a grin plastered on my face, filled with warmth. I had the feeling I had been pursued since my life began, and now for the first time, the pursuit was ended, and I could lean back, and remember the pursuit, from this vantage point of safety. I spent my days walking the leafy suburban streets, going to the corner store. Everyone told me how well I looked. Everyone thought I was in a great frame of mind. I didn't really have to work, because Cinderella was supporting us. I assumed she was doing this with the money she got from alimony. Until one night I woke up about three or four AM and heard the front door closing, looked out into the living room, and saw her standing there with three Japanese businessmen. They all smiled at me, and she said something about them to me that I didn't hear, and something about me to them that made them laugh deeply and harshly. I went back to sleep, bathed in the mercurial colors of the TV screen, that shifted around like reins being pulled up or let to fall, and when I woke up, she was there with a fruit punch in her hand, that she wanted me to drink.

I said, "Was it a dream, or did I see three Japanese businessmen here last night?"

"Oh, come off it," she said, taking a drink of the fruit punch, a green drink. "Don't you know where I go every night?"

"I didn't know you went anywhere at night, except for last night. Why, where do you go?"

"I go on *dates*, silly."

She was swirling around in the kitchen toasting pop-tarts. "How do you think I pay for this house, and the payments on my car, and *your* insurance, and the phone bill, and on and on...?" she called to me from the kitchen.

"How much did you make last night?"

"Six hundred," she said, put a Fiesta Ware cerulean plate on the bed beside me, on which were two warm pop-tarts, and kissed me on the side of the face. Then she set about the detailed unwrapping motions required to bring the heroin and all its accoutrements out into the open.

I left soon after that, feeling that I had unwittingly become a pimp, and didn't really want to continue taking her money. It was too great a responsibility. However, I could not say I disapproved of what she had been doing for money, because I realized she had become hooked on this expensive drug during her marriage, and there was no other way she could have earned the massive amounts required to keep her habit going. When we started talking honestly about this aspect of her life, it came out that she also did a lot of things like get her car fixed, or have expensive dental work done, all on the barter system. She had several drug connections, among the many she knew, who would always give her a few days' supply in exchange for sex. All this information, I found, was very exciting to me, and I liked asking her what they said to her, what she said to them, and all those secret details, while I was in bed with her.

After I left, I called her one time to try to buy some dope. She said she wouldn't be home, but the dope would be on a certain bureau in her house, I could come and pick it up. When I got there, there was no dope (besides myself, of course) but she *had* left a poem, on the spot where the drug was supposed to have been, and I read it. It was a poem about suicide, a veiled threat of suicide. When I asked her about it later, she acted in a way that I thought was very strange. She denied that she had placed the poem there, she insisted the *dope* was there... All in all, it seemed like a bad time to leave her all alone, so I went out to her place and we had a long talk. We decided she would come live at *my* place, and we would no longer take drugs, either of us. We also decided that she would give up being a prostitute, and we would try to get by on the money I was about to receive for a screenplay.

I found that I had almost no withdrawal pains at all, just a little sniffling and muscle-aching, lasting about three or four days. Since I'd been taking heroin daily for several months by that time, I thought Cinderella must have been right when she told me there was no such thing as addiction. She didn't seem to be having any withdrawal symptoms either, although I later learned that was only because she never actually stopped taking the stuff. As for my own lack of pain, I have since heard the same story from others - that the first time is a sort of "freebie," - to fool you and make you think you can start all over again, and there will not be consequences. When, a year or so later (long having been separated from Cinderella by then), I started taking heroin again, and then tried to stop after that time, I found I was addicted.

A Queens lawyer, convicted of stealing money from his clients, has been fined $389,000, which will be distributed to his victims. He has also been sentenced to 15 years.

A woman is singing on the radio.

Now a man is singing.

4:11.

"Nice couple of days coming up... Patchy fog burning off late in the morning. Low 70's..."

"I fall into her arms, I help her with her clothes... And she knows the hell I'm going thru, in this world inside my head... There's a devil in the Bottle, and he wants to see me dead..."

This is the country station.

"Amanda
Light of my life,
Fate should have made you
A gentleman's wife..."
Waylon Jennings

"There's no use in going over
All the things that took
me under..."

Men making love to shadows, men making love to bottles, making love to guitars, love to sand, love to cars... But what are these love songs? Love is actually just a thread on which songwriters string their true fascinations, which all are linguistic. Love is lending its name to the rhymes, hoping its benefit will somehow radiate throughout the lines of these very clever songs, to soften what would otherwise be pretty brittle plays on words...

Now Jerry Lee Lewis comes on to lift the low spirits of our slice of the New York metropolitan audience, singing, "My name is Jerry Lee Lewis and I'm darned sure here to stay," causing me to wonder - Is he making some kind of reference to the fact that Elvis Presley is dead? Is he saying that he, Jerry

Lee, has no intention of dying young, like Elvis did? We know Elvis was his only rival. He was arrested a month before Elvis' death for crashing his car through the gates of Graceland, Elvis' home, screaming "I'm better than you! I should be richer and more famous than you!" I think of that now. "I'm sure here to say..."

There's some blue in the sky. I'm watching for the dawn breezes.

5:05. 5:06.

At 5:05 - 5:06 this morning, a previously still nighttime sky took on a touch of blue and a slight breeze began to stir, which right now is moving the branches of the trees in the courtyard, and all is sweet. The odor of sweet flowers, and the young, newborn leaves. I have just returned from sticking my head out the window.

I had a lady cabdriver today from Brazil, whose name was Olivia Sulino. She had the cleanest, most well-kept, spacious, gracious checker cab I have ever seen in New York. She has no plastic barrier between herself and the passengers. I suppose she doesn't drive at night. In most cabs, with the windows that only open half-way, and the bulletproof plastic divider closing you off from the possibility of any view through the cab's front window, you feel like you're in the lockup, waiting for the state to assign a public defender to your case, but in this cab today, Olivia Sulino's, you feel like you're on the moving terrace of a flying living room. She asked questions of me, like: "Is that N.Y.U.?" (It was the N.Y.U. library), "What nationality is that restaurant?" I told her it was Chilean.

Then the cabdriver I had tonight. He had white hair, a white complexion and a toothless grin. We were friends before I got into the cab because I had been loyal to him, and he appreciated it. I had hailed him from the right hand side of the street on 7th Avenue and 50th Street. He was in a left hand lane at the time. As he came down 7th he tried to move over into the right lane. But another cab, to the right of his, came speeding down the road, and did not allow him to get over.

This second cab therefore reached me first and came to a halt at my elbow. However, I walked away from it, and waited for the original cab, because he had been coming for me. Unfortunately, he told jokes. By this I mean not that he would speak, and in the course of speaking, would discover possibilities for the exercise of humor; but that he resorted to ready-made jokes, ready-made by himself as he drove around, looking for passengers to try them out on.

The first words out of his mouth were: "Hey, did you hear - Doctors just discovered in 1978, there's no cure for stupidity!"

When I failed to respond, he said, "You get it? They discovered in 1978!"

Weds. May 16. 9:08 P.M.

When he sees a girl, he says, "I'd like to give it directly to that girl."

So what? Is this chaos, or order? Is this a reusable copy of nature? It was surprisingly easy at the dentist's today. The most difficult thing at the dentist's office is answering questions about why my books are not being published. It has gotten so I can't wait to have the clamps in my mouth because they make it unnecessary to explain my failures.

Thurs. May 17. 2:58 A.M.

Dinner alone at Sandolino's, a yellowish-lit place, where I read the papers. Then to the Blue Parrot, to have a beer and watch the girls sitting bent forward, having their naked backs rubbed by men with thick mustaches. Slips of girls, in silk dresses, some with very long legs, wobbling around on high heels. There was one tall girl with extra-abundant hair. I stared at her, trying to gauge whether or not her eyes were looking at me behind the large lenses of her glasses. Unable to know, I sat on the bar stool until my beer bottle slipped gracefully out of my hand, down between my knees, to the floor, where it shattered. I stepped gingerly over the broken pieces and went home, not bothering to look for that girl's eyes behind the too-reflective surface of her lenses. I did shrug my shoulders and say, "What do I need this crap for?" in vain hope that she would follow me out into the street, calling "I hate that place, too," but she didn't. I think those girls, a lot of them, are students at the Parsons School of Design. I'm thinking of taking course there this summer in life drawing. My aim is to revive the painting style of the Italian Renaissance, the last time humanity was given its due. I regret the fact that I gave Susan the nude photos I had of her and watched her tear them up! The memory of her beauty in those days, may be my sole heir - the one number I have on entering a foreign city - and so on excitedly -

I was thinking yesterday, as a matter of fact - how it was that it took a couple of weeks, or more, even more, until I realized the irrevocable nature and insupportable magnitude of what I had lost when Susan finally called off our extended courtship. I mean, we had been together for several years, and had often called it off between us, but this time, it was forever, and that was the thing I realized only about 2 weeks after the actual fact, incredible as it may seem. I was slow. Since that realization did arrive, I have followed a strange pattern of action in my attempt to regain something of her. First, I tried to find women who were the same build and with the same hair color, as she had - then, I tried to find girls who dressed in a similar style, and finally, today, I find myself with girls who are the same age she was, when I met her. And they're getting harder to find.

Keep to the Middle Path, the Golden Mean, says the *I Ching*, my secret mentor. It says: "You have seen your nose, feet and topknot cut off. Not a good beginning. But there will be an end to your troubles."

This city is not giving enough to us. This made itself clear to me today...

There was the crawler, on 6th Avenue, once again in front of the supermarket. He is dressed in a filth-encrusted suit - but a *suit* - with a tie, with a filth-encrusted *white* shirt - and he crawls on his belly up & down the Ave. of the Americas, looking as though he were crossing the terrain beneath flying bullets.

Then there's the old woman who darts from trash can to trash can with the bullet-like, bee-like directness of a woman whose every movement is accompanied in her head by its own background music. You can almost hear the orchestra of her internality play "Ba-ba-ba-ba-barroop!" as she hotfoots it diagonally across the walkways of Washington Square Park from one basket of trash to the next, looking for food... Yes, for food, not for the newspapers, and not for thrown-away quilts and posters, or bits of furniture - She rummages under the newspapers until she comes to a brown paper bag, which she pulls out and rips down the side in a single motion, well acquainted with the quickest most efficient means of determining and extracting contents of these bags - like a smart raccoon in a human settlement.

Then you say: No, New York is the place where all the weaklings of the world can survive, weaklings who wouldn't last a year in a small town, or even a city with eyes enough to see who exists within it - but they can hang on in New York - New York is the place where drunks go, where men who have given up every form of mortal struggle still choose to struggle with the elements, rather than conducting their bumhood in some warmer or friendlier place.

You go around and all you see are people chewed up by the process of living we have in this city. At each stage of life, one foregoes graciousness, in order to achieve some greater goal, or just to hang on by the teeth in New York. And this hanging on, in New York, can be like being a little mite, establishing your civilization on the bottom of a camel's hoof. And the Greater Goal, so patiently worked for, often is not achieved. Savings were impossible, rents rose, vacations were needed, you went into debt because you believed in the sense of yourself that somebody gave you in a moment of misguided love or enthusiasm, and here you are, sixty years old, no money has been saved, you possess remarkably few items of value, and only your apartment knows you, that is very nice, of course, but is too much like the inside of a clock - and you will soon be forced to retire, but you haven't saved enough money to retire. What do you do? You've been betrayed by your society. It had nothing to offer you, but it promised much. You started out struggling, to get a foot in the door; you finally were in, but the expenses of the job and the expenses of the family were confiscatory - you are standing on 60th and Madison, covered by the trappings of leadership in our city - you are a figurehead - you are, and your jacket is, the model for all these younger men, carrying mirrors from their truck into the Pierre Hotel. Some day they may wear your worried look. How attractive it is that the bags under your eyes seem to have been dropped and anchored at the bottom of hell ... you bite the ledges inside your mouth. Who can you kill? Or, you could slip the clutch altogether! Why not? Run every credit card past its limit, borrow money from the bank, spend it all and then depart this world. "Yes," you are saying to yourself, "as long as I can kill myself, I'm in the driver's seat. Any time I want to I'll cash in and that's that. It's all downhill from here, unless these bastards give me enough to get out to the country and out of the god damned maze! By the breezes blowing at your back, you know the light has changed.

Did my Grandfather become ill, and die, because he had retired? He didn't know what to do. No, but didn't he know *we* all needed him. He must have! I hate these theories about people getting sick when they retire. Now my Mother is retiring, and she's very sick. Her leg hurts all the time. Her back itches. She's always tired. Why? And why should my Aunts, also both be ill, at the same time, and in much the same way? Is it really sugar that has done this damage to an entire generation? or is it butter fat, or starch - or nothing we eat, but something we breathe, here in the New York region? The answer will probably be discovered by the husband-and-wife team that digs up the remains of our civilization in ten thousand years. Maybe it's something in doctor's offices we are allergic to.

Later, that same morning...
Ta-*weet*! Ta-*weet*!
Bropudu - bropudu - bropudu!
We are in the park.

Although there really is no "in" to this park at all. At best, there are places beneath trees, slats of wood. It is a city block like all others, except with structures implied instead of actual. It is ringed around by joggers from N.Y.U. One beautiful blonde is going by. She must be in the Sociology Department. Here comes a black girl with a Swarthmore college sweatshirt. Does that description do her justice? If she would care to slow down for a few seconds, I could expand upon it. As it is, let me only say her pants are black and her shoes are yellow and blue. Here come two Austrian mountainclimbers, but they are walking, slogging at a slow pace, through the pulsating walls of runners coming toward them.

A diseased squirrel, black with torn fur and white splotches of flesh showing through. It looks at me. No food, pal. I threw it a dime, which it picked up in its cute little paws and put in its little mouth prep. to twitching off.

How could Swarthmore be back so soon? Her pants are not black, but green, her shoes are not whatever but green and brown. Unless she changed behind my back. Well, that's what we're here for - to sharpen eye-hand co-ordination, in case an event should one day take place that I will have to record as it happens.

Facing the inner circles of the park, oblivious to the joggers, are those who have slept in the park, or, if that were impossible due to the ability of the police cars to reach any part of the park in an instant, they have come to the park from wherever they did sleep, to catch the first sun, first available in wide-open spaces like this. The joggers are mostly in shorts and T-shirts, but *these* men and, in the case of two or three, women, wear many layers of clothing, everything they own, probably, in the way of sweaters and coats. One of the men is already drunk, waving a brown bottle around, laughing and lifting both feet off the ground and smacking them down again. He is one of the youngest of the men there. He has silvery hair with remaining clumps of the original color - yellow - and he has it combed carefully in a gigantic pompadour.

Friday. May 18. 4:09 A.M.

A girl named Grace Gold, 17 years old, in her first year at Barnard, was hit on the forehead last night by a piece of concrete falling from the outer wall of a building up near Columbia. From her picture in the paper, you can see she was a beautiful, sweet girl. The article in the *Post* talked about other recent victims of falling objects in New York. One woman was hit by a safe, one man was hit and killed by a descending chair. The most celebrated case, said the paper, was the barbell that fell from the window of the apartment of T.V. stars Martin Gable and Arlene Francis, hitting someone on the head. It was determined that the maid had loosened the barbell, which was being used to prop the window open, in her attempt to clean, or water, the plants. Martin Gable and Arlene Francis agreed to pay $185,000 to the family of the victim.

I was sitting at a table full of people I didn't know, in the University One Bar about an hour ago, when one of the women - Louisa - said something about the incident of the Barnard girl. Everyone knew about it.

"Only the good die young."

I had been thinking about that saying, in relation to the girl's death. She did seem to be, among the people of the city, one of the good ones. And she is only the most recent, it seems to me, of a long, long string of cases, all of which have been in the newspapers, and which could be used just as easily to illustrate that proverb. It always seems that when some girl is raped, and then murdered, in a very brutal and terrible way - she turns out to have been the nicest, most wonderful kind of person - one who has been working to support her parents and family, going to school, doing volunteer work - or a young honor student who has a paper route is killed trying to protect his week's receipts from a couple of punk crooks in the subway, or in an empty lot somewhere, and dies between yellow lines, for under ten dollars, never to grow up, or have the rewards of life, but just to be dead, while his killers will live long enough to forget his face... Why? Why so many good ones dying young, and why so many good ones dying young spectacularly, in a newsworthy manner?

Is it that our city, like every ancient village, sacrifices a certain number of its finest youths? Could it be that, though we don't know even the names of our local gods, even though we don't pray to any local gods, as they do in the African forests, and in all the towns of Asia - could it be that nevertheless there are local gods, who take their toll instead of homage? This might explain the spectacular and horrible nature of certain deaths. It is almost as though these "local gods" want to make sure our attention is drawn to certain deaths. As though these are designed as exemplary deaths, to call the minds of all who read about them, or see them on the news, to the dangerous nature of life, "nimble misfortune," and send bolts of fear throughout our bones. In my case - they have succeeded.

Or you think:

Is it because they're so *good* that they had to die?

If so - don't be too good.

Always leave room for improvement. Operate on the theory that you will not be killed off until you are totally *good*. Therefore, be bad.

Should the full proverb say: "The good die young, and the old die good."?

The most important use for science, we do not use. The most important use for computers, we do not use. We should study the case of every person who dies accidentally or by violence. We should ask ourselves if such deaths can be seen as the final stage of a kind of process, or course of disease, just as death from cancer is the end-result of a history of cancer. To determine this, we might have teams of interviewers to visit every relative and acquaintance of people who die by accident or violence. They should ask questions about every aspect of the victims' lives. Perhaps they will find some common characteristic. Is there a sentence each one may have said the day before his death, or the week before. Is there any way they all were feeling? Had they had dreams, had they had premonitions, had they done something completely inexplicable two weeks earlier? What kind of structure is really around us? We have no idea. We don't know, except by rare sparks of instinct, how to behave in regard to the world itself, apart from the people in it, who are after all only its emissaries. We do not know how it sees us. Most of the time we do not know it sees us at all. The basic premise of science is that the world is *not* trying to tell us anything; therefore, for a long time in order to tell us anything the world has had to behave as though it were not trying to tell us anything. To those peoples who believe the world is talking directly to them, the world behaves completely differently. Have teams, tracking down evidence - feed the data to a computer, and let's see if there's something we have overlooked - a straight line that may be drawn through all the cyclical occurrences.

There is my jacket, which I tore tonight on 13th street, after we dropped Jane off at number 32. What was I doing with my arm so close to that cast iron bannister? If only there had been some way of foretelling that, I would have changed my actions somewhere much earlier in the evening, if need be, to have protected that sleeve, of the only jacket I like to wear.

I wonder if the only thing that links all the victims of these violent deaths is that, two or three days before, they put a small tear in one of their sleeves, just like that one. Dawn has come and gone. 5:26 A.M.

A. Phillip Randolph has recently died. He started the International Brotherhood of Sleeping Car Porters - he led the fight to obtain employment for blacks in industry during World War II - and to desegregate the Armed Forces after that war - He organized the 1963 March on Washington - He died in a "modest apartment on 9th Avenue and 27th Street..."

Columbia University owns the building from which the chunk fell off that hit Grace Gold, according to WINS news. Water had seeped in behind the concrete and gradually loosened it. The spokesman for Columbia says those buildings are well cared for. What kind of spokesman would he be if he said anything else?

Jane, the girl we dropped off at her home, is an actress. She has been the girlfriend of a famous video director and multi-billionaire, and former boss of mine. Jane had blonde hair swept down over her forehead and flipping up at the end at a point directly in front of the centers of her eyes. She is very attractive. She was wearing a cowboy shirt rather loosely hanging about her making visible her round breasts from where I was sitting. I put my hand on the back of her chair and patted her back or shoulder a few times. How can I describe her face? It is somehow Mayan because her nose is broad & flat. Her eyes are blue, however. I agreed with her that *Manhattan* was a terrible movie. Somehow, she soon realized I have not seen it, but she didn't seem to mind. I have an impartial love for all women these days, but even among them, I place Jane in high regard. Her waist is thin. I put my arm around it for a few seconds. James mentioned that I had worked for her boyfriend, Armand Lasovich, adapting a novel into a screenplay. He egged me on to tell her what had happened. What had happened was that Armand put me up at the Algonquin while I wrote the script, and that by the time I turned out the script we were on bad terms, so when he paid me the final installment of the money he owed me he deducted $500 for "overeating." For some reason, this and similar stories about my experiences with Armand, made her eyes glitter. Maybe they're having a fight. Still, you think: Who asked her to be the slave to his master? A lot of these women act like they've been indentured out to the rich, or as though it is their duty to some principality of peasants to form an alliance with the local Duke.

I said when I knew Armand he wore sunglasses at all times, and drank vodka from the bottle, from the moment he woke up. She said he's much more conservative now. James said for the first three years he knew Armand, Armand was the one in the cowboy hat lying on the floor. Jane objected to this kind of talk about "one of my beaux." We walked her home. I asked her if she wanted to walk me home, or take me to her home. She said something I didn't hear. I said, What? She said, "You heard me." Now I can't decide if she said something good or something bad.

What is this I'm watching?

I thought that was a dog, but now it appears to be a goat... Now what? There goes a siren down 15th Street, not stopping at 7th Avenue, not turning, going West to the Hudson River...

The dog became a goat
The day became remote
The air molecular did seem
Then I saw men
Without a Captain
Perish in a fiery stream...

Saturday. May 19. 6:21 A.M.

A depth of rain pitches down upon our courtyard now - upon the fire escapes, the white cat, the tortoise cat, their bowls, the ping-pong table covered by a clear tarp and two stones, the ancient columns and more recent fire plugs in the architect's garden, through the newly abundant leaves, and through the dawn itself, like a crowd of people rushing through a narrow slit of a doorway.

Sammy tumbled for 200 dollars worth of very good stuff.

My eyes blur and then refocus with greater frequency as the days pass on.

This was a good night. I had a feeling it would be, from the moment he brought me what I wanted. I was able to prevail upon him to deliver it to me at my place, with the promise of a date, for Trace had called and asked if I would have dinner with her, and a friend named Sam - a girl. When she got here with Sam, I was immediately suspicious that Sam might be, or might once have been, a man. Her hands were large, her neck was muscular, and she had some certain mannerisms of the two transsexuals I have met. When Sammy arrived I took him aside and asked him if he thought Sam were a man. He was embarrassed. He had been attracted to her. I had not realized this. Once I did know, I said, "Oh, I don't think I'm right." However, this attempt at qualification must not have set his mind at ease. I'll ask him tonight. After that, we couldn't seem to think of any restaurant that suited him. He said he had to be at the Village Gate by 10:15, and left us on the Avenue of the Americas shuffling off down 8th Street in his black leather sports jacket and narrow tie. T., Sam and I went to the University Bar.

I questioned Trace on her relationship with Papel, whom she met through me. First she had met him years ago, when I was still going out with her friend, then, she had met him a few weeks ago, when she was going out with me. He called her behind my back, and she went out with him. He's rich, handsomely fat, brown-haired, and has a great big smile. According to Tracy, she has seen him a few times since the night we all went out together. They have slept together a few times, but have not made love. She seemed puzzled by what was going on.

"I'll spend the night with him, but he won't do anything."

"Well, is that because you won't let him do anything?"

"He's not very demanding."

"That doesn't sound like him, are you sure you're telling me the truth?" I asked with a smile. Why shouldn't she?

"I guess he just likes being with me. I think he likes me because I'm the only person he knows who isn't impressed with his wealth..." (This after telling me about his Gulf & Western stock) "...I'm really not. Pssh! What's it to me? And he can sense that, I think."

I said, "Sure, why should you be impressed?"

T. has a straight posture and a slow take, on all things said to her. She sits there. She looks *somewhere* for a long time before speaking. By "somewhere" I mean were her eyes looking into my eyes, at my nose, at the air between us, or at the smoke of her cigarette? She finally says: "Although - I *have* been thinking about it, and I really hate this whole work thing. I mean just knowing I'm going to have to struggle to earn a living, for the rest of my life. It's so boring. And I do wonder - isn't there any way out of it?"

"Sure - you have to marry someone with money. That's the way it's done."

"And that's why it's done," she said. "Really - it's always been that way too, hasn't it. In every society. The woman's supposed to marry the richest man she can find. The most eligible bachelor." She wasn't embarrassed. She knew I was being a spoilsport, but would not acknowledge my right o be one.

"And eligible means rich," I said.

"Right, know anybody?"

"Well, I've already introduced you to Papel. I want you to know that I do think you shouldn't have gone out with him, since he was a friend of mine." I was reacting in an infantile manner to what I had learned - that she was sleeping with round, juicy, Papel.

Now I look behind my shoulder here, and gaze upon the little face of Trace. She is asleep. She is wearing my blue plaid shirt. What slivers of eyelids. You can't be positive with women... I shld. simply tell her she's a bitch & a whore for going out with Papel - instead I deflect my anger into unworthy remarks - I try to manipulate her feelings while maintaining the illusion of impartiality. Or does she want me to get angry, does she want me to make various demands whose only possible outcome, should she accede to them, would be that the two of us would be committed to one another. She *did* ask me, earlier on, what my right was in concerning myself with her social activities.

Now, I move the covers.

"What are you doing?"

"Touching you."

"I mean with your other hand."

"Writing my diary, about our conversation at the University Bar."

Sat. May 19. 10:30 P.M.

We went over to University One, which was the second time last night I was at that place - which all say looks like a dim cafeteria of some college. The owner presides in a red v-neck collegiate sweater, and all is well. They take checks. Artists go there. Students from NYU, if everywhere else is closed... T. gave her number to a singer. We left, Lenny drove Trace and me to my home. T., Corey, and I sat in the small back seat. I put my arms around Corey and asked her if she ever wore stockings and garter belts. She said she usually wore pants. I said that was terrible. She said she was wearing stockings tonight only because her dress was slit up the side, held together by safety pins at the hips and she wanted to at least have something on. When we got here, T. got out of the car first and I kissed Corey goodnight. To my surprise, she gave me a long kiss, which led to another. She said, "Call me when you go to Massachusetts." We had discussed the possibility of driving up to Boston together, so I could visit my Mother, and she could visit some friends of hers on Martha's Vineyard. I said, "Don't you ever come into the city?"

What next? It is now 11:02. Should I go to 10th Street now, or wait for Arthur to call, and go with him? Wait.

Sunday. May 20. 3:02 P.M.

I Ching promised me a girl I could get along with, and when asked to put it in a time-frame, said one month. That was one month and a few days ago. The big problem is, I took it seriously.

But what am I looking for? Who needs them?

Got to the party last night, somehow ended up in the unoccupied loft directly below the one where the party was, with Corey. She told me she has talked about me with her old man. The fact that she has told her boyfriend she likes me, and the fact that she told him she would sleep with me, the fact that he doesn't give a flying fuck, and the fact that they "discuss everything," all these facts make the prospect of an affair with Corey slightly less rosy than it originally appeared to me. I like Corey. I think I should leave it at that. Although, we do know he wouldn't care... Yes, but what one needs is not any part of their wonderful scene - it is one's *own* scene...

The party was given by two male models, twins of Greek origin, whom I did not meet. They were good-looking & tan. The trouble with these lofts is that half of them always wind up looking like a garbage dump. This one was a dump of collector's items, like World War II posters, large cardboard cutouts of diesel engines and cars of the '40's & '50's.

The Phone.

"Hello?"

"Hi, Sammy."

"No, that's OK."

"I'm not sleeping, not busy..."

That was Sammy. His habit must be getting serious. Now *he* calls me... He even makes an effort to be nice! The rabbi's son has raised the price of his tenths. James wanted to know if I wanted anything, as he was going over there. I said No. Now, I regret it. Should I call him back?

I'll ask *I Ching*.

I have a headache, because I drank too much last night. What a week: No more going out! No more people whatsoever, for one week! Eat only Chinese food, dream in peace.

"That's My Boy!" with Dean Martin & Jerry Lewis is on. This is the film that introduced Eddie Mayehoff. "Listen to that crowd boo!"

"Junior Jackson is running the wrong way!"

I have just pressed my eyelids and seen two universes of crosses of Lorraine, receding into the infinite blackness.

"Junior Jackson is being carried off the field on the shoulders of his teammates!"

"OK, Pal?"
"OK, Pal."
What would Wilhelm Reich say about this?

Monday. May 21. 12:24 A.M.

Robin called today, to see if I could help her get a job. I told her I had no idea where she could get one. Her response was to ask me, in an accusing tone, didn't I have this job, that job? I told her exactly what I did have - I told her that my book has no publisher, and so I have no publisher to send her to, for a job. Stupid bitch. She's still seeing the bald boyfriend. Catching the unmistakable sound of disinterest in my voice, she started fabricating causes for joy. She said, for instance, that she and the boyfriend would be going to Switzerland for the summer.

LATER

I have often felt that I should display I should display the power to earn money, and try to be doing well in my career, because women are so appreciative of these qualities. However, the result is that women who are interested in that aspect of things are attracted. Let me rather be totally broke, and meet a woman to whom that will not matter.

Let me also lay off that *I Ching* book! There is no doubt that when you ask it questions, you do get answers, from some sentient, intelligent being, but what is the purpose of that being? Why is it saying what it is saying? Several times, the same thing has happened to me with the *I Ching*... It tells me something will happen - during the night, or during the next month - then the thing does not happen - then I ask the Book, why didn't it happen, and it tells me to Retreat, to Withdraw, to be at Peace, but it never admits to having been just plain wrong. Of course, then you say to yrself - well, it just doesn't exist - It lied - or something - I was crazy to believe throwing coins would answer my questions - But then it strains itself to new heights of clear communications in order to defend itself, and to assure me of how ignorant I am... Then I flip out, tear it up (I have just torn my *I Ching Workbook* into trapezoidal shreds. I told it: "The way you look now is the result of the frustration you've caused me!") ... then I return to it forlornly, to ask new questions, or add more objections, try out new angles on it. I should give it a break. Enough is enough. It started 6 years ago, as a scientific experiment. I remember that guy who lived next door to me on Dudley Court. He had a green paperback edition with a circle on the cover. He was a paraphernalia and candle merchant. He said most people like to use the *Ching* only on important occasions, or once a month, or less often, but that he found himself consulting the Book about once every two or three days, about some business matter or other. He was very happy with the results, he said, and taught me how to throw the three pennies, six times, and read them to see if you have seven, eight, nine, or six, a straight or broken line, a changing line or not. At that time, I was living on the floor in a pink barn on Dudley Court, I was writing in the mornings, and I had all day to lay around and throw coins. At first I kept a record of every question I asked, and the figures of six lines, called hexagrams, that constitute the *I Ching's* answers to your questions. After the event occurred about which I had been asking it, I would check to see if the answer had foretold the true outcome. What I generally found was the answer *had* been correct, but it had been correct in some way no human could possibly have understood - even after reading its answers - so the result would be that all my questioning had not helped me, but I was still forced to admit, on careful re-reading, that it had answered correctly.

It has a habit, after putting me through a cycle of false hope followed by dashed hope, of introducing a new course of false hope. I feel this is so you'll stay hooked on the Book. You'll forgive it all the uselessness, all the frustration, in exchange for this new bright hope. You think, I must have misunderstood. I did something wrong. It was my fault. I'll stick with the *I Ching* until Thursday. I'll give it one more chance. Then along comes Thursday, but after you jump up & down on your personal volume, it says something like, "I'm your friend," or "You need my help" and promises the fulfillment of some wish, by next Saturday. Many years of your life can go by like this, and I have asked it on more than one occasion if it was the devil. Sometimes it says yes. Or at least it appears to say yes. Then, I ask again, and it says no.

I have just asked it if it agreed with my story of it, but I do not have any idea if it answered.

The answer was Hexagram 64, lines 2 & 3. Then I asked again & it answered, Hexagram 39, lines 3 & 6. Who knows? Right now I'm inclined to believe there is nothing behind it at all, beside the random falling of the coins. I'm so sick of the damn thing, I can't express how I hate it. Oh, to be able to find & strangle the spirit or spirits responsible for so much confusion, spread from my thoughts throughout the irregular palette of my endeavors.

Oh, you don't like that! Well - come through and I won't hate you!

Sometimes I don't ask questions - For instance, just now, I said, or rather, thought, (for I mutter my imprecations entirely inwardly, except when I get too excited): "I hope after I'm dead people read my indictment of you, and don't use the *I Ching* for 600 years, for all the uselessness of you!" It told me to be more modest.

"There is a sanctuary in New Mexico that stands on a fountain of mud that bubbles up through the shrine, and this mud is supposed to have miraculous healing power... The Indians worshipped this shrine of mud before it was converted to a Christian site... And that's today's story on...

"The Unexplained"..."

"WNEW 1030 New York"

"The time is 2:43 A.M."

Now we are listening to the theme song from "Picnic." I remember my Grandfather said William Holden would never have to worry about money, because he had it all in trust funds, that would pay it out to him over the years, thereby lowering the taxes he had to pay, and assuring he wouldn't spend it all at once... My Grandfather heard that in an interview with William Holden on late-night radio... He used to tell us these things while he made our lunch and packed it for us to take to school. He would wake us up by saying "Time & tide wait for no man!" or "To be or not to be, that is the question!" I only understood the meaning of the first one. The second one sounded important, but what did it mean?

Monday. May 21. 1:08 P.M.

At last I have a bit of normalcy in my hours. Went to sleep around 3:30, woke at about 11 A.M.

Edward got back from the Cannes Film Festival last night with some very good - but not as good as he said it was, or worth the $80 he charged me for it - stuff. But I have to stop this spending on dope. This living hand-to-nose has got to stop.

Monday. May 21. 2:35 P.M.

Just talked to Robin. I called her almost entirely thanks to a chain of suggestions given to me by the *I Ching*... And she was in a good mood, just waking up, having her coffee. She said she was going out to do a few things. She had a job interview. I asked if she would be down in the Village at all. She said no, but she could be. I said, "That would be great!" Then she said, "How about tomorrow night?" I said, "Wonderful! That's great!" I said, "I'll call you tomorrow afternoon to confirm." She said, "Or, if I'm not home, I'll call you." This part went on too long, now that I think of it. It had the sound of a plan that was destined not to be fulfilled. Try to omit from future conversations.

Sleeping on last night's fight with the *I Ching*, i awoke with this thought: Maybe, the reason it keeps giving me Hex 40, line 3 - saying I am a pretender to power I do not possess - is that I have been guilty of overly concerning myself with the sex lives of my girlfriends when they are not with me. Of course, that is true, and all the humiliation it had predicted yesterday would overwhelm me, did overwhelm me. Who am I to worry about Robin's friend? What right have I to be pissed at T. for her relationship with Papel? These things are none of my business. Now, I banish this trait from my groaning personality.

I read an article by Jerzy Kosinski, in the *Times* this morning, about how he goes out at night, in whatever city he happens to be, and he goes to some hospital or old peoples' home or poor ward, or other place where forgotten, lonely, people are, often those who are dying. He introduces himself to the head doctor of the place, or whoever is in charge at night, and shows a cover from one of his books, as identification. Then he goes to the rooms of people, and reads to them, sometimes from his own books, sometimes from the books of others.

Now I'm ashamed that I have not better appreciated this man's books. I never thought there was enough in them. Now I'm sure this impression was caused by the compression he exercises on his material... Unfortunately, compression is a hard thing for a writer to prove.

Monday. May 21. 8:45 P.M.
(Time Approx.)

"Loose joints. Check it out. Loose joints. Check it out. Something for your head?... Grass, hash, acid, ludes, coke, and pills, what do you want, how do you fills?"

You feel you can smoke a joint in the park these days not only without being arrested, but without being noticed. Still, when the motorscooter policeman came by, I put the joint in my pocket.

This is a temperate night. We have a group of soccer players, including one girl in a brown T-shirt, several frisbee throwers, and various bike-riders. We have round balls of white-satin light illuminating certain crowds of leaves, which look as though they are stuffed around the insides of various domes, the domes described by the force of the electric lights. Eerie vaults above the walkers and riders. Sometimes a loud group. Many couples, looking at everything from their perches on the concrete circle.

Monday. May 21. 10:23 P.M.

Something strange is on the radio. Four men are going to kill Death. They want a treasure chest, and expect Death to be guarding it.

"Where is the moment when the spirit is free?..."

Now they're burning the victims of the Plague. Because the ground is frozen and you can't bury them. They don't stop at the dead bodies, as the one called Gibb tells another, because by the time they're being burned, Death has done his work. They must look elsewhere for Death.

They go to a town which is lovely enough, but Gibb can tell the Plague is coming, so they stay...

Hold everything! This has just become too strange to follow... Here comes a leper through the streets... "No, it's Jeffrey, the Thief..."

I have called Sammy and Edward, and left messages on both the machines. It would be wonderful if I could get some junk for my date with Robin tomorrow night... She likes it. The *Ching* tells me to harbor no expectations and make no demands, and there will be good fortune. Be like a cork on the ocean to take advantage of the waves, the invisible current. What else can you do? You have to live in fear of accidents and malice. From your point of view, it's all accident. Even the malice of the earth is an accident, but these old Chinese sages did not look at it that way. They said you could plot the path of fortune through time - to know when to act and when to refrain from action, to know when the truly unavoidable thing was upon us, and when it could be avoided, and to know when you were earning your suffering through wrong thinking. Take it or leave it. They used to cut their question into a tortoise shell and then heat the shell with the point of a stick. If the split in the shell occurred at an angle of about 45° to about 135° from a reference line that had been grooved into the shell, the outcome of the event would be favorable for the inquirer. If the crack was less than 45° to more than 135° the result would be unfavorable. In one of the *I Ching* Books they have reprinted a "map of chance," which is like a string drawn through a maze in a newspaper, except that the main path often breaks off into two paths, one ending only a few centimeters from the main path, so there seem to be a series of nodes, or buds, standing out at certain places along the branches of change, as it travels around in the rectangle which is represented as its total shape.

Tuesday. May 22. 2:44 A.M.

There I was, when last in possession of the passive mood, and when last upon this geologically crimped sheet, before you, my digital friend, and the phone, as only it can, rang. It was Sammy's friend, the Photographer with the suntan. The last time I was at Sammy's, the Photographer and I waited together through the endless hours while Sam went across to the East Side, and the Photographer said that Sam got all his really great stuff from him, the Photographer himself. I remembered the great stuff, and asked what he had sold it to Sammy for. It was half what S. charged me. Therefore, I asked him to call me if he found anything else. He said, tonight, that he's had something good for two days, but only just remembered me. He said it was as good as Sammy's is these days, and was *less* than half the price - $200 for a half gram - 400 for a gram. I got a cab to Bank street & he gave me a large sample. It was good. We took a cab to the Citibank automatic teller, my downfall, which has allowed me to get money when I'm most susceptible to the worst temptations, at night, and I got the money - Then we took a cab to East 5th street and he ran up to get it. He was back in a moment. We took the cab, which we had kept during the time I got out and the time he got out, back to his place. The driver was a crew-cut kind of crazy one. I asked him if he minded being asked to wait, keeping the meter running. He said it wasn't very profitable for him, so I said we'd give him an extra tip.

When we got to Teddy's, the meter said $4. I gave him $7. He said nothing. I thought he was overwhelmed by my generosity. Instead, when I looked in the window at him, I saw him shaking his head, laughing to himself and talking under his breath. Then in disgust he threw the cab into gear and zoomed away. Why? He had just been telling me it was a slow night - he was having trouble getting fares - and here was a tip almost 100 percent of the fare! What did he want?

Then we went into the Photographer's apartment, where he has an Ohaus scale, and he discovered we had been short-weighted by a small amount - half a tenth of a gram out of the entire gram we had bought. He said he would give me my full share, and get his back from the man. He shot some up and started eating a hot fudge sundae. I snorted some - more than I have for a year, because I had so much, the price was so low - and started to nod happily. Then I looked at his photos. Recalling that James had expressed doubt as to whether the Photog was indeed a Photog or if he was a dealer exclusively. In fact, his photos are beautiful - he has a great way with beautiful girls jumping, acting tough and threatening, in the accepted modern manner of showing feminine beauty. One catalog he designed and photographed for a Japanese clothing designer must be a masterpiece of the Catalog, and say what you want about the transience of fashion, still - he constructed an astounding work of art, or so it seemed to me, who had every reason to love him at that moment and may have been somewhat off the path of true objectivity.

Now, as to the question of this drug-taking, or rather, as to the question of whether or not I should be including it in these digital notes of these days, and the answer to the question is: I must. My desire is to write down the full details of everything, during these days. I am told to, so as to find myself, by my childhood self.

I wake up in the A.M.'s with a terror previously unknown, of the poverty that yawns ahead of me, when all my money is gone down that interminable chute, and terror of the physical discomfort I have ever reason to expect will soon thereafter haul itself up through my flesh and nerves, the creepy skin, the hot & cold, the self-hate, the eternal presence of the self's less well known parts, less well known because less loved, less worthy of our companionship - those aspects of me will tell me their story, while my body sweats and aches, and while the ranks of ants shall sweep through the lower dermal areas of me. So, I do know and realize the results of this path, and how much what is good, is bad; how much all that furthers me in this endeavor,, actually prepares me for suffering. Yet, I can not help but be grateful to the Photographer, for sharing the good fortune of this inexpensive find with me, one whom he does not really know. Yet he likes me, and I like him. He's honest. He says he lives with two models - one has just quit a job as a topless dancer, because she doesn't like the new custom at the peep show places, of allowing the men watching to reach in and touch the girls. I was hoping to see the models when we got back to his place, but they weren't there. Where he lives, a number of transvestite whores hung out on the corner. It is right across the street from the majestic Hudson River... The Photog said I could come over and sun myself in their garden. He has kindly eyes. However, when his eyes are pinned from the junk, his pupils recede to a spot from which they seem to regard with skepticism that spot which, if they had not receded, they would occupy in space. Now I have a solid bunch of junk for when Robin comes over tonight. What! Thinking of bribing the beautiful Robin? Thinking of exchanging drugs for sex? Yes. Will I suffer for this slip in sensibility. The idea is to learn from James. Everyone loves modesty. It's like a painting. Don't I myself seek James out to talk with? Of course, sometimes you get the feeling he's not giving enough. He is reticent on many topics. Therefore, I end up doing a lot of yammering, leaving me feeling slightly exposed, as though I had proliferated the evidence that one day would hang me. But then I consider him objectively, and I see the modesty radiating from his clear face.

Humility makes up for almost every human failing, the lack of humility diminishes every good quality. This being the case, I pray I learn humility soon, before it is taught to me.

As of now, I have apologies to make to Robin, to T., and to Corey - To Robin and T., for pretending to rights over them that I didn't have, and to Corey for storming out of the B & H Food Shop a few nights ago without giving her so much as a peck on the cheek, or a smile. I just couldn't stand that place any more - that light - those sizzling blintzes - I was drunk and bored. I wanted to walk. I needed air...

But I should have taken my leave with the full realization that I was leaving sensitive people, and that transgressions are liable to spring up everywhere unless you are as careful not to transgress as you are not to starve.

As for myself, I fear the lack of humility has been deeply planted in the turf of my skull crowded in there along with the candles of self, casting its own weird shadows over all my actions - I say senseless things, I say things that I have no way of knowing will be offensive, but which I manage to say to the one person in the world they might offend. I make feeble jokes that cause people to cry, or leave the table where I am. How sick I am of the drama in relationships! How sick I am of the crises I seem to create, and of all the begging for forgiveness I do... I have often, often, returned home from a pleasant day, only to sit bolt upright the second after my head hits the pillow, full of shame or dread, over some remark I made during the day, which I suddenly realize was not only misplaced, it may have been sub-human, savage... Then I walk back & forth, until I can calm myself down by telling myself I will never again speak without thinking... I also try to think of the proper apology, or, if the offense is so embarrassing - or if it was some confession, or accidentally displayed attitude that I know marks me as a villain with the one before whom I told it - I try to think of ways never to see that person again.

On my way home tonight I saw the man who sleeps on 7th Avenue on the subway grating of the I.R.T.

He is there every night.

He has a long, filthy beard and is wearing a brown suit and dark shoes.

One night I saw his ankles, between his exploded shoes and the cuffs of his pants. They were black with soot. He is a thin, intellectual-looking, white man. He looks like a film historian who has decided to give up the constant effort of earning a living by teaching and writing.

Tonight, he looked at me as I passed, an amused look on his face. He was lounging on the ground. Leaning on his left elbow, looking out at the passing world, as though he were watching it from a bay window.

He was smoking a cigarette in an opulent manner.

He lies near the wall of the bank on the corner of 7th Ave. and 14th Street.

4:48 A.M.

I should hit the hay. Make some zees.

What about looking at *Playboy* or the Lord & Taylor catalog and jerking off?

I wish I had a copy of *Seventeen*.

I do.

And a copy of the June *Glamour*, which Elaine told me to get, because she's in it.

Amazing how the camera captures the sun-touched flesh. Here's a girl looking out at us. She's sitting on a floor covered with hay. She's drinking a glass of champagne. Perfect realism, just the beverage for a barn. Here's a picture of the same girl without any shoes. She's wearing sunglasses. The sun is touching her outward-pouting flesh areas. She is picking up a stone from the beach with her bare toes. Having wonderful time.

Tuesday. May 22. 9:22 A.M.

Just been out for the morning walk. Ate eggs. Managed to find every street where there were no beautiful women.

A man with no hands has escaped from the prison ward of Belleview Hospital. He is a bomb-maker from the FALN - the Puerto Rican Liberation Front - and his hands were blown off by one of his own bombs. I saw him in an interview they re-ran on the occasion of his escape. He says: "The press and the media release the information that my face has been blown away, that half my head has been blown away, but that isn't true. They just say that to put fear into the people. It's propaganda."

And he said, "No jail can hold me!" and now he has proved himself to have been right, in this case. The police are understandably puzzled as to how a handless man could have ripped through the steel mesh covering the windows of his room, and then lowered himself three stories... They are investigating the possibility that he had help.

10:08

My method is archaeological.

I believe that once the attention is turned on, then a search is conducted, the duration of the search is like the area of an archaeological dig, and that if I label and tag each moment, like a cube of earth taken from a finite pit, it will from then on be available for scientific examination - to learn what? Who knows? To learn if this is a real or a mythical city. To learn if such things as I see are fact or legend - and so on - and so -

I made an archaeological discovery a few minutes ago, as a matter of fact. I discovered a note I wrote a month ago.

"How can I express it?" I expressed myself, "Two nights with Robin, and the weather turning warm - early morning on York Avenue - her shaggy dog, her gray-blue eyes - last night she cried when I wanted to leave her, to go and work. We watched Columbo, an old movie, and the Alfred Hitchcock Show.

I remember when Robin was getting close to me, but I pushed her away, I had to finish that book about Wilhelm Reich. What would Reich say about that - giving up sex to write about it? I had lived 30 years and accomplished nothing - I had to have one thing done. She said she was lonely. She started telling me about all the rich men she was meeting. I was deaf to her warnings. Now, I have only the slim hope that humility will win her back from the arrogant, well-to-do preppie I was reduced to chatting with, during those last days, when I was going over to Robin's because she had a source of heroin. I would only stay to hand over my money & get the stuff. He, the preppie, standing, tearing lettuce for salad, or chewing a radish. I was not allowed to tell him what I was there for. Robin doesn't want him to know she is acquainted with junk. He thinks I come over to talk to her about putting her in a movie.

Tuesday. May 22. 8:12 P.M.

Laura. Gene Tierney. Waldo says: "I'm not kind, Ambitious. It's the secret of my charm. But if you choose to think me kind, I'll call for you at six."

Cool oceanic evening over 15th street. Many dogs and children wending back & forth.

The *Ching* says I can forget about seeing Robin tonight. Good. I have no desire to share my junk. I'm back to sleeping from late morning to early evening.

The Photog. calls & says the good variety of dope, called "Grey Elephant" is now in town. Unfortunately, the *I Ching* doesn't want me to get any. Could be dangerous. Attach itself to me. I'm taking the advice, unhappily, but with a sense of rightness. I *must* stop!

Absolutely, right, Ching!

Robin just called. I was sweet as could be. She cancelled.

But. She wants to come over tomorrow. 9:30.

Weds. May 23. 3:14 A.M.

I'd love to skip the dentist today.

Thurs. May 24. 1:43 A.M.

At 11, I went out with Brian just in from Toronto. We talked about the animated film I am writing for him. That is, I would be writing it now, but he and his associates in Toronto are supposed to create the outline first, for me to work from. They have not been having much luck with the story. I've already spent most of the $5,000 they sent me on the signing of the contract, and I'm not supposed to get paid again until after I hand in a 40-page treatment of the script, which I can't start until I get the outline. I'm afraid if this drags on too long, they'll decide not to do it at all. Then how would I pay for all this dope? There are my shoes with the buckles on them. They are walking towards the moon-walk shoes I got when it was snowing. I finally got 20 hangers, a few days ago. Now, I have all my suits, jackets, pants and beautiful bathrobes my mother made for me, all hanging up. I should have called my mother. I'm holding a grudge, it isn't right.

5:18 A.M.

One thing I have been taught by television is that the human face is composed of many figure 8's. Figure 8 for the eyes, figure 8 enclosing the forehead and the lower portion of the face, passing perpendicularly through the figure 8 that links the eyes. There are also two diagonal figure 8's - each of whose lower bulbs is a cheek of the face, and whose upper bulb is that side of the forehead which is on the opposite side of the nose from the cheek enclosed by the lower bulb. There is an 8 whose lower bulb comes down along the sides of the nose and whose bottom is the bottom of the chin, and whose upper bulb describes an area of equal, or almost equal width between the frontal lobes of the forehead. Then of course there are the 8's going in several directions that comprise the nose and the nostrils. The ears are eights. Also, it seems that *eight*ness (the quality of being able to expand the top and bottom circles endlessly while keeping always the same center and the *eight*ish shape) is much responsible for the abilities we have of opening and closing our mouths, or our eyes, and of making all kinds of facial expressions. There is also a system of 8's keeping the back of the skull attached to the front, and the neck joins the head and body in a nest of 8's ... and also the body, and all its parts seem formed of an endless number of 8's, many eights enclosing smaller eights, through a rotosphere of various bodily positions and positions available to each part of the body. The 8's of the forearms, of the combined forearm and hand, of the fingers and their corresponding segments of the top of the hand, and on and on excitedly, as I forget what I was...

Oh yes! The way everything seems to be like an eight.

Also in Nature, in the shapes of animals and insects, of flowers and leaves, and even (all evidence suggests) in the shape of the winds and waters, are many eights - in ocean currents and storms, and the way water seems to link hands at obstacles, curving arms around them to join up later - all have the 8ward way. Also, candles, flames, all fire, flickering upward takes that shape, as it turns around and around itself, and rises by crossing and re-crossing itself, until by such crossing and re-crossing it is changed into other elements, and the tendrils of these other elements are waiting for the tendrils of the fire, reaching crossed arms downward as the fire reaches crossed arms upward, to be drawn up, like a person rescued from the sea, into the arms of a different state of matter...

So might it also be true of structures over time? With the fates of people?

And might it also be
that every doom and destiny
Crosses itself
And then goes free?

End of Book II.

Book III

No matter why I get angry, my Mother will tell me I'm not really angry because of *it*, but because of something that happened to me 30 years ago. This is because she believes in the efficacy of psychology. When my brother was born, and my mother went to the hospital, I was taken from home to my Grandmother's house. According to my Mother, this dislocation was too much of a shock for me. I felt she had deserted me. Because I couldn't talk or understand, I was unable to complain, and therefore I have been angry about it to this day, and it is the secret cause of my irrational outbursts. I really have never thought this incident sounded that important, but who knows? She tells me I refused to look at her after I came back from my Grandmother's. I liked my brother right away, but would not forgive her. Now that I write it down, it occurs to me that perhaps my characteristic suspiciousness, and my unforgiving nature, were not brought on by the short stay at my Grandmother's - perhaps that only brought them to light for the first time. Perhaps I did understand pretty well what was going on, but only used this incident as a chance to be mean. A rotten kid. However, if she thinks all my impertinence has its origin in this ancient trauma, that's probably a good thing.

I should call her. It's up to me to carry on the original vision. A family. I remember when I used to get on the phone to my mother, get on the phone to my father, then back to my mother, my father, etc., to try and negotiate a deal for him to send her some fraction of his unpaid child-support payments. Who are these people? I appreciate everything they did, but why didn't they give us a break? Couldn't they have subsumed that self-indulgent drama for the benefit of their bewildered sons? Oh, shut up, Mabius, you ingrate! She subsumed her whole life for us. I should call her. Would she have been happier without kids? I don't know. I remember I used to think, How can I be better? How can I be good? For one day, at least. But it was impossible.

Thurs. May 24. 5:34 A.M.

I am in heaven... It is a rain-slaked dawn today, and the causes for my being in heaven, or noticing that I am, are the sounds - the cars, the generators, the spoon against the metal pot across the courtyard, the hollow gurgle, the clearing throats in the clearing, and thanks to the slight breezes of dawn, the rustling of the leaves outside my aluminum window. The leaves are the kind used as models for chocolate leaves. There went a bus...

I have looked out the window, put my elbows on the window sill, and taken many deep breaths. The white and tortoise cats are not on the fire escape opposite me, or lurking around the food bowls kept filled for them by the woman in the garden apartment next door. I was actually able to see someone, to the right, two buildings over. He (I think it is a man. Either my vision is failing, or he's standing behind a very thickly layered window, so greasy it's as though someone rubbed a stick of butter over it.) Well, man or woman, he's shelling peas over a large pot. The sound I heard before is evidently his pinky ring banging against the side of the pot. Now some birds are starting up. Seems late for them to be starting. Maybe not. 5:52. Now I'm nodding out. Good for me.

Friday. May 25. 1:41 A.M.

I went to the Photographer's garden apartment at 9 tonight. The place was packed. Three or four British rock musicians, a little French guy, the two models who live there, the Photographer himself, looking like an old-time flash attachment has just gone off in his eyes. This stuff is too good.

It's brown. I guess that's why they call it "grey elephant." The old Photog is taking so much he goes through doors like a submarine rookie during his first depth charge attack. His pupils are only suggested by the convergence of blast-lines at the center of the blue of his eyes. There was a new girl there. She was quite a large girl, with blonde hair in a pony tail, wearing a dress that was open to show her breasts, crowded together in their polka dot cradle, and she had on a pleated skirt that clung around her hips and ass. When I came in, she was cooking her dope in a spoon. Being so solid-looking, blase, and a little unfriendly, even to the slim guy who was evidently her escort, she gave the impression of being the wife of a man whom she did not think earned enough money, and who is on a trip to a shopping mall with her husband, and is dissatisfied. She was bent over the sink, to fill a hypodermic with heroin, water and a bit of citric acid - which is necessary to use with this particular junk, in order to get the powder fine enough to get into the needle - with a leather belt wrapped around her right arm to force blood into her lower arm, and force her veins to swell. I sat down to wait for my bag to be weighed out. I sat in such a position as to be able to watch the girl. She was talking about a modelling job she has tomorrow - "runway" modelling - a kind she has never done, so she was nervous. Laurette, the French girl, told her not to worry, just to try not to fall down... Others laughed at the aptness of that last bit of advice, but the beautiful girl didn't. The girl just tapped her right arm with her left hand as she held the syringe between her teeth. Then she tried to insert the needle into one of the veins in her arm. She was unsuccessful. She had to pull the needle out of her arm and rinse the blood off, in a coffee cup, then try again. This time she tried to get a firm base for her work by leaning against the refrigerator door and putting one foot up on the counter across the narrow kitchen from the refrigerator. She was wearing black stiletto heels with little white socks, such as Corey was wearing the other day. She couldn't seem to find the vein. She was so exasperated she started blindly rotating the inserted needle, poking at various angles, pulling the needle slowly back & forth like a violin bow, so that in case she had gone too deep, and passed the vein, she would be able to catch it on the way back. By the time she got it, blood was dripping from her elbow to the floor from three puncture wounds, as though from 3 open faucets. Still, she took her time. She double-registered, twice. That is when you inject half of the junk into the vein, then you pull the plunger back, to fill the transparent syringe with your blood, mixing it with the remaining junk, then you shoot half of that mixture in, then pull the plunger out again, then shove it back in again. However, this girl did something even more nerve-wracking. She pulled the blood-filled syringe out of the right arm, and plunged it into her left arm, which had all along, unseen by me, had a rubber hose wrapped around it to prepare the veins. The legs, ass, and infinitely disinterested face of the girl impressed me. The brew that she had sent barrelling through her veins was evidently attacking her brain from both sides at once. I winked at her and she cracked up laughing.

Anyway, let me look around that room a moment more... Is there anything else to say about it? No.

When I was going to school in Baltimore, I lived with my friend, Jack, on Calvert Street. Our apartment was on the top floor. One of its features was that you could sit outside the windows on the tar rooftops.

After the assassination of Martin Luther King, there were riots in Baltimore. We watched the riots beginning, on T.V. The next day, I decided to go downtown, to see them. I heard that black people were running through the streets, breaking the windows of stores, and stealing massive pieces of furniture. It sounded exciting. When I got back to my area of the city, after being beaten up a couple of times, I saw the girl who lived in the basement of our building. She said, "You better hurry home, you know - there's a curfew."

She had a little, childish face, framed by a fifteen-inch tall hairdo of light blue hair, with a streak of absolute white running up one side like a part. "Oh, I don't care about that stuff." I said.

"The cops are stopping people, they stopped me, too," she said. "I know them all, though."

She said she worked as a go-go dancer on Greenmount Avenue, a street with three or four nightclubs, a few blocks from where I lived. I said I had noticed her hair, and thought she might be in show business. She was wearing a yellow mini-dress, white vinyl boots and dark brown pantie-hose. We walked on, past National Guard troops marching, and sirens in her honor, from passing police cars, until we realized we lived in the same house! She had a separate entrance, because her apartment was in the basement, and we had never seen one another because her hours were different from mine. We sat on the steps, talking, until she suggested that she bring some strawberry ice cream upstairs for us. I ran upstairs to tell Jack about the girl who was our neighbor. I said, "She's incredibly nice, really sweet, but for some reason, she talks very slowly. Try to figure out why."

After our ice cream, and a conversation that was less smoothe, having three people in it, Beverly invited me to come down to her place and sit with her while she tried to go to sleep. As I followed her out the door, Jack touched the crook of his elbow with the forefinger of the opposite hand, and said, "Reason for the slow speech? Look at her arms."

"Her arms?"

"Her arms. Unless I'm mistaken, the mosquito season hasn't started yet. Look at her arms."

When I got to her little basement room, however, I didn't have to look at her arms, because I could watch her fingers, as they sharpened the point of a needle against the flint strip on a book of matches. She had a glass of water, a blackened tin spoon, a ball of cotton and a mound of white dope on a glossy magazine cover.

It was the first time I had seen anyone using heroin. I had read about it, in the books of Wm. Burroughs, but still, it had no reality for me, until that night. Beverly said, "I should have warned you to hold on a few minutes. See, I didn't have a chance to do this before, because I wanted to hurry on up with our ice cream, but I just gotta now, hon - is that alright?"

"Sure. Absolutely."

"Mmm. Feels good," she said.

Then, when she had gotten the dope into the syringe, and I had been watching her every movement with total concentration, she said. "Maybe you better not watch me while I do it, hon - "

"How come - does it make you nervous?"

"Me? No. It's just that - well - you might find it a li'l sick'nin!"

"I can take it!" I said.

Beverly's veins, in her arms and legs, had been assaulted so many times that they had retreated deeper beneath her flesh, fearing the needle, or collapsed completely. Therefore, there were not too many places she could get a shot into herself any more. She showed me the holes between each of her fingers, between her toes, and in her neck, the last of which were covered with stage make-up.

"Well, I give up," I said, determined to be cool, "Where are you going to inject it?"

She had gotten up & gone to the mirror on the bathroom door.

"Behind the eyeball," she said. Beverly carefully inserted the point of her needle between her eyeball and the socket that enclosed it, and, when it was in there, to her satisfaction, she shot the junk behind her eye.

Then, she was in a great mood, singing, clapping her hands for a few seconds, then, she said, "Jeez," and sat down on her bed. She patted it for me to sit down, too. There was a thin clear line of water coming out of that inside corner of her eye, down her cheek. She told me she came from Virginia. Her father owned a small ranch that was always in economic trouble. She had married a boy in Virginia, who was in the Army. Then, he was stationed near Baltimore, so she had moved there, to be with him. After a year, though, he was sent to Viet Nam, and he had been there now for three years. I told her how afraid I was of having to go into the Army, and especially of Viet Nam.

"He eats it up," she said. "They made him a Lieutenant, so he eats it up."

"Does he know about your taking junk?"

"Sure. He takes it hisself. He's th' one got me started in the first place! But he's supposed to be sendin' me some, ever' week or so, a little bit like, for me to you know, take a little bit, and save the rest, for him to sell when he gets back. We could be gettin' ah-sel's quaht a liddle nest-egg, 'cept he ain't sent but one time.

"That's why ah gotta dance for a livin' in them naht-clubs."

She said she also made money dating men. She said she didn't sleep with them. She didn't have to, because they would pay a hundred dollars just to be seen in a restaurant with her, or for her to hang around at a card game. They were gangsters.

That night I tried some of her dope, snorting it instead of shooting it, and we talked about Virginia, her father's ranch, my own life and hopes, my future books, and the strangeness of things, that it had taken a riot and martial law, to get two people acquainted who lived in the same house. I liked her. She was working out a plan for withdrawing from drugs. She would even give up dancing, and just go on her innocent dinner dates for a living, with those mysterious old men who, it became clear after a while, were also the suppliers of the junk she took.

After that, we would see each other every now and then, but not often. Three times I saw a limousine, late at night, and the driver would go around to the side of the building and fetch her. She would come out and cross the deserted street to the car, then wait for the driver to open the door for her on the street side. She was always dressed in a glittery sheath and high heels on these occasions, and carrying a feather boa. Once she saw me just as she was about to get into the car, and winked at me, and threw a kiss.

Soon afterward, it was summer vacation, and Jack and I left the city, for different places. By the time we got back, for the Fall semester, I had forgotten about Beverly, or at least I wasn't thinking of her. About the third day back, I met our landlord in the front of the house supervising his son, who was painting the bannister of the porch. It was a nice day. He left his son alone for a few minutes to talk to me.

He asked if I had known the girl who lived in the basement apartment.

I said yes, why, had she left town? He said, "She was a hooker, you know. I didn't know it when I rented to her, but she had men in there all the time. Did ya ever talk to her or anything?"

I said, "Yeah. But I don't think she was a hooker exactly. She said there were certain men who paid for the privilege of being seen with her, at lunch."

He looked crookedly for a while, then said, "Nah, she was a hooker! Whaddya mean they paid her to eat lunch wid her? That's what she told you? Really?"

"She was a junkie, too." said our landlord. "I told her a couple of times I was going to have to kick her out of here if she didn't stop, but *they* can't stop, they can't *stop*, so what are you going to do? Put them out on the street? Did you ever see her refrigerator? Nothing but ice cream. I'm telling you, cartons & cartons of strawberry ice cream..."

I thought, what is this?

"...They can't stop. She couldn't. That's why she's dead..."

"What do you mean, dead?"

He gave his head a minute click to one side like the double-take of a comedian. "I mean *dead*, dead. She's gone, you know? Dead. They found her body under a bridge out in Reisterstown. You didn't hear about this? It was in the paper, and on television. You know what it was?"

"What?" I wanted to lean against something, but every available surface on all sides of me was covered by wet black paint. I was thinking of Beverly, dead.

"She was moidehed," he said. "She was caught in the middle, and they had to kill her." My landlord was sad about it. Had he been in love with Beverly?

What had happened was that the old man in the limo prevailed upon Beverly to let him pay for her breasts to be reshaped, so that she could do runway burlesque, in which the dancer is right out over the audience on a long strip of stage running through the theater. While she was in the hospital, however, the police decided it was a perfect opportunity to find out, from her, all about the old man in the limo, and his friends. Since Beverly was a junkie, they knew they could get her to tell them everything she knew by withholding her supply of heroin, or threatening to. They moved her to a "secure" area of the hospital and placed a police guard at her door. After the police had interrogated her for one day, that night she disappeared from her room. The policeman who had been on guard said no one had entered or left through the door, and there were bars on the windows. The guard did admit to having gone to the bathroom one time without first telling the nurse on duty. A week later, Beverly's body was found. She had been shot in the head.

My landlord said, "She was a sweet kid, though, you know? It's a goddam shame."

"Did you ever meet her husband?"

"No. I met a couple of her boyfriends, though. Nice enough fellas, the two I met different times."

"But why would they have to *kill* her?" I said, not meaning the boyfriends, but the old man in the limo, and his friends. "Couldn't they simply have given her some money and sent her out of the state?"

"I guess they figured they could never count on her. They couldn't be completely sure she wouldn't get arrested again. She probably would, you know? And then it would be the same thing all over again. All the cops would have to do is cut off her supply. She became too dangerous to them. I don't know what she may have known, but whatever it was, I guess they didn't want her to tell anyone about it."

And that was the story of Beverly Everly, returned after many years to my mind by the seeing of that girl at the Photog's. Laurette, his girlfriend, was cooking him some liver or steak, very domestic, looks out at me from the smoke & fumes, sees these models plugging needles in their arms & legs, and says: "Eez a shooting gallery here, no?"

Laurette, it seems, liked hitting me up so well last time that she asked if I wanted it again. I said OK, although I didn't really want to shoot it, because I prefer the feeling when you snort it. But I like her, she is pretty, and I like it when she ties my arm with one of her polyester stretch belts and then spits on the crook of my elbow just before she jabs the needle in, to raise the vein up. She loves to push and pull the blood in and out of the barrel of the needle, until you say, "Enough! Stop! I feel it, I feel it!"

Sunday. May 27. 5:02 A.M.

5:08 - First chirping of a bird. Look outside. Already plenty of blue in the sky. Still the lone bird. What is he saying? Sounds like the muezzin, calling us to morning prayer.

I have just returned from the end-of-the-season party for the cast of the Night Line Show, which was held on the skating rink at Rockefeller Center. When I left they were still dancing. Tried to call Robin earlier. First no answer. Then the bald actor answered a couple of times. I didn't feel like talking to him so I hung up. The second time I said sorry before I hung up.

Sunday. May 27. 2:55 P.M.

That was a brilliant entry, that last one. It put me to sleep. But when does this sky get light? Light! Light! More light! Sorry, G. - limited light. Limited light, and limited warmth are upon us now, as our ancestors could only have guessed at! Call this "The Sorrows of Young Mabius." The difference between me and Young Werther is that he had someone to write his letters to. This is going to be one of those days... Maxwell House, so perfect for emulsifying yesterday's food. I don't want to take any junk until I absolutely have to. I must lower the level of it in my blood. $2,000 in the last three weeks for dope, and I'm not even getting high most of the time. Now I'm out of money and I haven't even begun to write the dialog for the rats to say. I will not receive another penny until those rats can chat for 90-100 minutes, as well as having things to do, pranks to play, dangers to escape. I made a great breakthrough with Brian the last time he was here, by suggesting that the hero be a mouse or a cat instead of a man. The fact is, Brian and his partners have found it impossible to make any progress at all w/the story and are hungry for any suggestion. Anyway, I wish I could remain at least fairly stoned through the creation of the whole cartoon. This way, it's bound to be a rather nervous comedy. I wonder how families all over America would like a film about a bunch of rats coming off a strong dope habit? Sounds English.

We are always inside an egg. The orgone field is the amniotic fluid...

The phone.

"Michael Mabius please."

"Speaking."

"Hi, Michael, this is Corey."

"Oh, HI, Corey!"

Monday. May 28. 2:35 A.M.

Sunday, and its attendant night, have turned out to be very exciting, very wonderful, all by dint of the things the amniotic fluid has colloided toward my locale. First there was the call from Corey. She said she was going to Virginia sometime this weekend and wanted to know if I'd go with her. No end of joy all afternoon, the thought of driving to Virginia with such a beautiful girl. Spring. Woods. Car crushing toward the South. It came back to me over and over. How would I get money and a car? I don't want to go by train.

Then, fresh from my happy telephone call from Corey, I started thinking of sex. That led me to wonder if I might have any luck if I went over to 13th Street and knocked on that girl Jane's door, the actress I met the other night at the University Bar with James. I took a bath, put on my best blue shirt, and went over to her address. On the way, I passed a crowd of people coming out of the movie on 13th Street. I saw their faces beneath streetlights and trees. I was praying for love, to its own god... I smiled benignly on the opposing horde. People are threatened if you smile, on the streets of New York. In Maine, they wave at passing cars, while in New York, it seems there is no interlocking looking. Plenty of looking, and plenty of looking away. Nobody looking, and receiving the look, and both frankly looking, which might then lead to talking. Many secret appraisals instead.

I got to Jane's. There were no names on the bells, so I rang them all. I called her name, Jane Jane Jane, to the little brick building with several lights on, and the curtains of the third floor blowing in and out. No one at all came into view. I walked on down to the Bar, and who should be there, but Jane. I did not speak to her. She was whispering with a girlfriend of hers and two thin men, and they were all making each other laugh wildly. That stopped me.

5:24 A.M.

I pray to many gods. I see them just above the lip of my eyes's cup of bone. Are they my Ancestors? Are they the former lovers of the Place I presently occupy? Are they the Spirits of my Occupation? Writers watching over writers? And if so, who are the spirits to watch over a new genre, a form with no Masters? Or does it stand to reason that the Masters of all forms are sick of their own Forms, and just as happy to supervise some new Form? Anyway, they are a multiplicity. I have no argument with the idea that they may ultimately all be answerable to the One, Our Lord, but perhaps that answerability is subject only to a periodic review? Some local spirit makes a decision concerning your life, and if it were unjust, or incorrect, The One might not know about it until it was too late to do you any good. There was an article once in the New York *Times*, about a series of interviews with people who had died and then, after being dead for a few minutes, came back to life. This happens 300 times a year in the U.S. The person says the pain suddenly stopped, then he was able to feel himself leaving his body, able to look down and observe what was going on in the room where he has died, and is later able to repeat things that were said while he was dead. The interviews were divided between people who had died in America and people who had died in India, (for some reason) and the result was that every American who died said Heaven was a wonderful place, Death was a great adventure, lovely, peaceful, filled with calm rivers, and their departed friends and relatives coming toward them with smiles on their faces. However, every person who had died and come back in India said exactly the opposite thing: Death was a horrible place, full of demons, pain and suffering. What could possibly explain this phenomenon? Could Heaven actually be a geographical thing, like the Earth. Does America have its own Heaven, face to face with it through space - rolling, every mountain on Earth an indentation on Heaven, every valley of Earth a hill of Heaven... One thing was missing from the report. I don't know whether it was just left out by the reporter, or if the scientists who conducted the interviews forgot to classify their data in this one important way. How did those Indians who died in America, and those Americans who died in India, find Heaven? I don't mean, How did they locate it, but what was their impression, although the question of how they located it isn't bad, either.

Tuesday. May 29. 2:31 A.M.

This is a great city, a great city. Too great for me, I'm afraid. Too great for anyone without benefit of a helicopter or a priest ... DOT DOT DOT ... DOT DOT DOT ... DOT DOT DOT... On the news tonight Pia Lindstrom told us an interesting fact: that of the 25 murders committed in New York during a single week suspects were brought to trial in 12 of the cases, and only 4 of the murderers went to jail, none on the charge of murder.

Rose is coming to clean tomorrow. Last week she told me about her son's trial, which is coming up soon. Her son is mentally retarded, as they say. He is 19 years old, but has never been on a bus or train by himself. He is afraid to be more than a few blocks from home. It seems he was standing on the street one evening a few months ago, when some boys came running around the corner, and one of them gave him a pistol, and told him to hold it. A moment later, a police car pulled up and he was arrested for possession of the pistol. He has never hurt anyone - Still, the judge wants to put him in prison. The judge is the same one he had a few years ago when he was arrested for shoplifting, with a group of his friends, and at that time, the judge gave them all suspended sentences, so now he wants Rose's son to serve a prison term for committing an offense while on a suspended sentence. It's as though the Justice System were a predator in the jungle - a lion, forced to live by catching the members of some herd, and devouring them. However, the lion is getting old, and the only antelopes it can catch are the sick ones, the lame ones, the slightly simple ones, so these it must slaughter and pick clean their bones. That's the way it is in a great city ... A town of renown... The man who sleeps on Seventh Avenue was standing erect this evening, when I went out for my hour in the air. He was holding a white wooden dowel. He held onto it with weak fingers, even as the owner of the Donut Shop was pushing him down the street. He stood loose-jointed, with his mouth open at the center of his beard, but it said nothing. He only appeared ready to speak. He dangled his thin white dowel like a child as the powerfully built Greek or Cypriot with downturned moustache shoved at his shoulder, that seemed to be a mound of hanging threads of black. This is the first time I've ever seen the outdoor sleeper upright. He is an incredibly regal beggar. The way he observes the people who pass in review as he lounges in his place on the sidewalk, where he royally toasts himself on the hot breezes from the subway beneath the grating on which he reclines; and now, the way he resists the pushing of the donut man. He makes it look like he and the donut man are working together, somehow - as though by the donut man pushing one way and his pushing the other way, they are both managing to stay at the exact spot where they are. You look at his face, and it's as though he were offering encouragement to the other, as though saying: "Just keep pushing - we can hold our position all night, until reinforcements come!" The donut man, not exactly devoid of quirks himself, was trying to act like the beggar's friend as he pushed him from his store's area. He kept saying, "I'm trying to save you, I'm trying to save you! The cops is coming and they'll get you if they find you here. They'll arrest you, they'll put you in prison, you don't want that, do you, you better go over there, go hide in the alley, go in the doorway across the street, ooh, here they come, I can hear the sirens, ooh, they're gonna get you, they're gonna, ooh, they're gonna do terrible things to ya, ooh..." I went into the store to buy some donuts and corn muffins, the only thing I can afford to eat now that Citibank has cut off my credit until my Canadian check clears. Of course, to hear Marty talk, I could ask him for a loan at any time, to tide me over. In the donut shop was a uniformed police officer, licking the powdered sugar off his blue sleeves before de-squatting from the round stool on which he was balanced. He didn't give any sign of caring about the 7th Ave. Sleeper. I stuck my head out the door and called to the proprietor, who was still struggling w/the sleeper, "Can I get something to go?" and he stopped pushing the Sleeper, and turned around. He said sure and came back into the store. He said, "Let me wash my hands from touching that garbage. Then I'll get your order, sir."

I said, "Terrific."

I smiled at the police officer, quickly looking at the wall display of naked donut pans, to avoid having him inspect my pupils too closely. The cop went outside and walked over to the Sleeper. "Here," he said, and threw the man a quarter. The Sleeper dropped it, picked it up, and wandered off down the street, looking at the ground, swinging the insubstantial white dowel lamely at his side... Dot Dot Dot... The *Soho Weekly News* offers a $500 reward for information about the missing child, who went to his school bus three mornings ago and has not been seen since. Rose comes from Jamaica, already two of her sons are in prison - What can a black man do in this city to get ahead? Sell dope... Dawn... I feel like taking a walk in this unresistant cool air. It is -

5:35 A.M., so -

There won't be any people around, for an hour or so, but perhaps I should sleep.

Tuesday. May 29.
9:59 A.M.

Editor's Note: At this point, Mabius decided to cut up an issue of a fashion magazine. The entry for Tuesday, May 29.

9:59 A.M. utilizes a picture of a digital watch cut from the magazine. On the face of the watch is the time, 9:59. Beneath the watch we see a picture of a young girl with long blonde hair, her arms raised above her head, sunglasses covering her eyes, wearing a green T-shirt and white shorts. The prices $3.57 and $5.96 are written over shirt and shorts, respectively.

On the next page (pg. 508 in the original notebooks) we have a large female foot, in a black-strapped shoe. Beside it are a much smaller photo of a smiling girl, again with blonde hair, and, beside that, a photo of a pair of girl's legs in a slit skirt. Beneath these are pictures of 10 diamond rings and what appears to be a human nostril, arranged at the same angle as the rings.

On page 509, we see a girl diving backwards into water, at the moment her arms disappear beneath the splash. She is young. Above her hands we see a pair of red lips, larger than the girl's entire face. Also on the page is what appears to be a long golden shoehorn.

On page 510, there is a full-page shot of the face of a blonde girl with green eyes.

On page 511, is what must be the hair belonging to the girl on 510, but it is pasted in sideways, and she is looking at it, instead of wearing it. In the sea of hair is a red plastic barrette.

Tuesday. May 29. 10:17 P.M.

Here I am waiting for the Photog. to get home, so I can stop getting that weary-toned girl whenever I call there. She acts as though you've got the wrong number until you have talked long enough to pass the rigid test of tedium she has devised for identifying authentic customers of the Photog. The idea tonight is to put together a deal so I can get a gram and pay the Photographer the $250 I owe him. Lance was over here before, but we had a fight and he walked out. Now he has just called me back to apologize and try to get me to go and get this dope for him. Lance, I now know, recently charged me $800 for some stuff *he* got for $200. He got it at the Cannes Film Festival and mailed it to himself in a letter. I suppose he felt I should finance his entire trip. He acts as though he went over there for the express purpose of getting me the dope.

Now, he says he doesn't want me to think about that. He's sorry he charged me so much, but says, "I get the feeling you're holding a grudge against me, and I want that to stop, so we can go on, the way we were before."

I said, "Up till now I never thought you were making anything when you sold me stuff."

"I swear to God, I never charged you a dime before this. I just thought, fuck it, even though I got a deal on the stuff in France, shouldn't I charge you the going rate in New York - to be fair?"

11:26 P.M

.

Now the Photographer is home. Lance has been notified and is racing to my address in a taxi with his money. The Photog. says this batch is running out. I wish I could buy up the remaining supply. The trouble with wasting your money is you don't have it when you want to waste it. Well, I'll get what I can. Instead of following my usual practice of apportioning the powder, a little for now, a little for later, a little less for the next day, I feel like taking it all at once - not only for the added rush at the beginning, but also because I want it to run out. I haven't had a dry day for a month, and I'm beginning to get numb. I'm never high, I never have that sharp discomfort the makes the subsequent intoxication that much more relaxing... The bell. I go.

Wednesday. May 30. 2:54 A.M.

Yes, he's really running out. He's trying to sell it all by tomorrow afternoon so he can send his cash to London and have a new supply sent over here. He recommends I buy a large quantity tomorrow. I wish I could, but the bank will not release my funds, probably for another week... I'll have to stop, that's all there is to it. Tell everyone I have a cold and lie in bed for a few days. Who needs it anyway? The euphoria is now minimal. It's like trying to take a deep breath, and finding you can't get your fill of air, you can't find the barrier, your head is out the window but there simply is no air, that's the way it is when you've built your tolerance up. It's the way you feel without any drugs. Stop, or get so much it will make a difference - so much you will be able to get high. It is raining.

4:44 A.M.

The street looks like a wet raincoat, black, with smears of yellow and red from the streetlights and traffic lights. The trees are nodding and flinching as the rain gets harder.

Thursday. May 31. 12:20 A.M.

The *I Ching* is incredible! It *knows*! I have been in its thrall for seven years now, growing more and more dependent on it, for the large and small decisions that come up every day - but still, ours has not been a smoothe relationship. I believe I wrote earlier about my tantrums, when I am so frustrated by some opaque area of inquiry that I often throw, tear or otherwise abuse the book itself. These texts I'm using now are about the tenth and eleventh I've had to buy. As a matter of fact, for two hours last night here I was, on this mattress, fighting with the *I Ching* over a certain point, on which it would not answer me... What happened was, about three or four weeks ago, I asked it if my Wilhelm Reich book would find a publisher *within two weeks* from the day I asked. Now, to my surprise it said "Yes." I don't write down the questions and answers any more, as I did during the first four years or so, but I'm sure it did say "Yes." OK. Then last night I asked again, will the book get a publisher soon? The *I Ching* wouldn't answer. It said, as a matter of fact, "The answer to this question will cause you trouble," and steadfastly refused to answer. Over and over I threw the pennies. I asked in every way I could think of. I craved a yes-or-no answer. It talked about my personality, my intelligence, my flaws, errors for improvement, and so on - it told me to stop, wait, be moderate, contemplate, retreat, be passive, build my strength for the future - Anything and everything except a plain yes or no.

Then I thought, maybe I was mistaken when I thought, weeks ago, that it *had* said I'd find a publisher.

I asked, "Am I correct in believing, as I do, that you *did* say the book would find a publisher in two weeks?"

It answered positively.

I was correct.

"OK." said I, "I was correct. You did say it. Now: is it true?"

Again came the evasions, and the famous philosophic advice, which can seem extremely cruel and pompous after a little while.

I finally cracked the code: "Do you mean," I asked, "you don't want to tell me, because if I knew the answer, whatever it is, I would do or say something *wrong*, just because I knew the answer to that question?"

That was it. Hexagram One.

I felt clever, having figured out the hitch, but I still wanted the answer. I pounded my head with my shoe... Anyone walking in at that moment certainly would have run out again. I am broke. The banks are closed. I want to get some dope. It's running out. I ask the *I Ching*, "Will I be able to get any dope tonight," and much to my amazement it says: Hex. 34 line 5: "The situation will progress with ease." Unable to believe this actually means I will get the dope - for after all, I have no money, and owe the Photog. $100. - I ask again. Again it says yes. This time, Hex 46, line 4, a good line.

"Ah-ha!" I thought - "Now I've got you!"

You have said that I shall succeed in obtaining heroin tonight, while I *know* there is no such possibility. My only source of cash would be *Lance*, and *he* made it a point, last night, after getting home and opening the stuff he got from me last night, to call me and tell me:

"Man, he's cut it. He's put a step on it. Either a one or a two, I don't know. The last time I got it, it was brown rocks, now it's a light brown powder."

However, I decided to call him, on the off chance. That was the occasion of the Miracle - No, he didn't want to buy any - it was too expensive - But he did want to know if I would like to borrow a hundred and fifteen dollars so I could get my own, and pay him back tomorrow? I took a cab to his place, got the money, all in disbelief. The *I Ching*, against all the evidence, had known the future truth, and had told it to me. Worse than that; fresh from the disappointment of adrenalin inspired by the Book's refusal to tell me what I wanted to know about publishers, I had latched onto the seeming impossibility of its doing prediction, and had said: "When this night passes, and I still am left without junk, then at last I'll be absolutely sure that either you do not exist or you do not tell the truth (an idea that returns now and then to me, when, after some long time spent in some certain expectation, raised by it, that expectation is not fulfilled, and then it tells me that I was mistaken in my interpretation all along) and when that does happen - " I said to the *I Ching*, with my pennies poised over its torn, coverless pages in a gesture of defiance, " - When that does happen, I'll finally admit to myself that ... *you are useless!"*

Then, of course, I had to admit I was wrong.

As for "The Search for Wilhelm Reich"... Perhaps it *will* be published, but if I knew that for sure right now, I might not continue working on the dialog for the futuristic rats, which is the proper current focus of my attention and faith. Perhaps it will *not* be published, but to be aware of that right now would cause me to cut my wrists with the Blue Star Single-Edge razor I have been using to cut pictures of girls and dogs out of magazines, along with diamond rings, walruses and a nose. The night is widening and widening until it disappears, and I can feel the generators start up in the office buildings twenty streets away, and hear the many-pressured sounds of the cars and busses, and lean out, as I have just done, between a couple of these commas, to take my ritual breaths, half of whose deepness is ritual, while half of whose deepness is for air, and see, as I have just seen, the elderly nun across the courtyard, to the right of me, standing in the kitchen of the Home for Friendless Women shelling peas into a gigantic steel pot, behind barred windows... In either case, I now am inclined to believe that the Book does know the answer to the question, and that it also knows I must not be told, until some later time than this.

But it is beginning to feel like I shall not get to the later times that I so much concern myself with the events and results of... At least, that I shall not reach my later times via *time*; that if at later times I am to arrive, I will do it by another way, which is what? Pure forgetfulness? Am I here standing guard, and will my life not change until I fall asleep, and allow the enemy to overrun me? But that is the very thing I cannot bear to do, because it fills me w/dread, as dry as a page of some discredited science.

6:41 A.M.

And what was it caused Lance to transmogrify from penny-pinching to wild generosity? He must have his own relationship with his own set of gods, and felt he must do it. I am high, but deep. In debt... Might have to forego the pleasure of answering the phone for a couple of days... Lance is probably right now asking himself why he loaned money, and will be back to his own self tomorrow...

Friday. June 1. 4:23 A.M.

Zero.

Friday. June 1. 7:18 A.M.

Hello? Dawn? Dark?
There's a ringing in my ears.
Answer it.

Nothing. Sleep.
Die. Eat.
'Scuse me while I cauterize.

Saturday. June 2. 2:08 A.M.

I was over at the Photographer's last night. I went with James, who was kind enough to advance me another $100. Laurette, the French girl, tried to hit me up with the needle I had just bought from her - thoughtfully provided for the customers - only $4 - but it was a fiasco. My veins were nowhere to be found in my arm. I wrapped a belt around the upper arm so tightly I will have a scar, but still, no veins appeared. I shook, jumped, clenched my fist. Finally, she plunged it into my ass, or "bum" as the English people present called it.

Rose called before. She didn't come today because she was looking for some kind of "program" that would take her son, so he will be allowed to avoid prison by the Judge. She was told to try Phoenix House. Marty has a lawyer who will help Rose's son, a lawyer who has devoted his life to helping poor people avoid the jaws of the law. The awful Law we have here, like a licking tongue of fire, slithering down every street, in through every door and window to find the cowering citizenry, in their inalert homes. Just leaned out the window to see the largest police van I've ever seen - it was like a Recreational Vehicle, but said Police Police and was in blue-and-white. What was it doing beneath my innocent ledge? Strange siren, too. Like a dying man trying to tell you who did it, but only getting out the first syllable of his killer's name, over and over, maddeningly dwelling on that first syllable.

I asked the *I Ching* if I should try to get any junk tonight. It said I'd succeed, and be able to get it. Then I asked if it didn't think I should stop this foolishness, and it agreed, so now it answers all questions on that topic from this new point of view, which is getting a little annoying, as I have slipped from my former resolve, although the Book still carries forward that original, principled aim.

A girl named Laura called tonight, and reminded me I had eaten dinner with her, and James, a few months ago. I invited her over and made the mistake of taking her out to dinner. Should have stayed home tonight... We got to the Elephant & Castle, where the waitress asked us to wait in the vestibule until a table was cleared off. We waited, then it looked like it had been cleared off, and we came in again. However, a very strange waitress started scolding us for having returned from the little vestibule too soon.

I said, "Well, the other girl said to wait until it was clear, it looks clear now, we came in," but this waitress said, "I'm still working on it, so you can just go back there and wait."

I was surprised by her tone, not to mention made rebellious, and decided not to move. I wasn't in her way, I thought. She said, "So - you're not going to obey, right?"

"Obey?" I said, "No, I'm not going to *obey*." Stressing the word to show her how absurd it sounded for a waitress, any waitress, to expect the diners to "obey" her.

We sat down after she had put the napkins on the table. Then she gave us menus, but would not recognize us after that. Finally, she said, "You didn't listen to me, now I'm not listening to you."

"Well, it doesn't have to be you, get us another waitress," I said. Laura didn't know what to make of her dinner companion. Should she have called me at all? She had her doubts. No service came. After a while I knocked a glass of water on the floor. It didn't break. The waitress kept a smile on her red face as she stepped over the water. She was showing me she didn't even notice. We sat there a while, until it was obvious we would not be served. The only thing left to do was to leave quietly, but I couldn't do it, I couldn't stand to do it. Instead, I unscrewed the top of the sugar shaker and told Laura I was going to turn it over on the table, so she should leave right now, and I would follow. She left. Instead of the dull act of turning the sugar shaker over, however, I decided instead to turn the whole table over, which I did, as I stood up. The water, sugar, condiments and candles, slid to the floor. I smiled at the Maitre d'. "I'm terribly sorry." I said. Then I tipped two chairs over and again said I was very sorry. As I left, I was lucky enough to be able to bump into our waitress with the door, sending her...

End of Book III.

Book IV

...sprawling from the vestibule into the street, on top of the group of girls she was just then telling to wait. She kept her smile the whole time, a smile of victory. For we had been driven away. I said I was terribly sorry when she turned around, grinning, to see what had hit her. Then we went to the University Bar, where I saw Jane, who didn't recognize me.

Saturday. June 2. 5:35 A.M.

Sunday. June 3. 4:27 A.M.

At 5:35 A.M. I passed out. First, my eyes went out of focus a few times, then my jaw started dropping away from my face, then my face, unable to locate the lines of the notebook, searched them out by leaning toward the book, until it fell thereonto, and thenceforth there did come to a stopping place, from which it did not move until about 4 this afternoon. Luckily, I had taken the precaution of replacing the needle and barrel in the envelope where I hide it, so it was not seen by Rose, or anyone who might have come in here while I was asleep, like Marty, who, in order to compensate himself for the great acts of charity he expects some day to perpetrate, sometimes comes in and takes some of my grass off the legal pads where I roll it up. Then, he tells me it was cheap stuff. All this passing out was the result of my decision to abandon half-hearted measures, and to try to get really stoned. I did. However, today it is apparent I made a mistake in so doing. According to Laurette, the French girl at the Photographer's place, they have been robbed. All the heroin is gone. The ersatz Raid Insecticide can in which they had all their carefully weighed-out packages of $50, $100, and $200 worth of dope, each in a piece of magazine paper, is gone. They sound awful on the phone. Laurette is in utter misery, it sounds like. She did manage to tell me she's figured out why she couldn't find my vein last night. The needle was too small. I had thought it was something my vein was doing. Still, it's very fortunate for me I did buy a needle, because now that my supply is limited, I can scrape my old packages for the powdered remnants of former warmth, and these amounts, which would do me no good at all if I sniffed them up, work quite well popped into the flesh.

Trace is here beside me, sleeping.

Trace and I provide one another, mostly, with our own pasts. Ten years knowing one another... No, fifteen!

The country station is on. The candle is burning. A slice of lemon lies beside the candle, in the saucer, with its pictures of roses all around the rim. Why don't I take another shot? 4:49. Why not? I feel so good why not feel better?

Very nice.

Now, to the business at hand.

When were the Hero and the Villain first presented as different people? I'm the New Classical Age; they once again shall be the same person.

Monday. June 4. 2:41 A.M.

It was touch & go for a while, but Laurette finally called me and after I had begged for it properly, they allowed me to come over and get some of the precious *new* dope they have bought, since the "grey elephant" was stolen. When Laurette is there, the Photog. defers all decisions to her, and spends most of his time w/his eyes shut. They're not selling to everyone. I had to convince her on the phone I was sick. I really wasn't very sick. I still had old papers I was scraping, cooking and shooting. If it wasn't for this little insulin needle, however, I would not have been able to stretch what I had to fill the necessary hours. I came back from their place singing in the rain, Down Bank Street. I couldn't get that song out of my mind. ("All these people that you mention...") I remembered when I first heard it when I was young, and my brother and I would sit in the beams of sunlight on the floor of our apartment, listening to Bob Dylan and our Broadway Musical Cast Albums. We had all of them - "Wildcat," with Lucille Ball, "On the Town," by Comden and Green, "Do-Re-Mi" with Phil Silvers. I'm heaving big sighs now. Yes, I am. For those old days, when we were back in those days, and my Grandfather was alive, and we all lived with my Mother, and she used to read magazines while we listened to those albums. We had a dog we used to play with on the rug, until the sun got so low the windows became opaque, filled with golden powder. Have I betrayed my family by what I have done these past several years? They aren't like this. They wouldn't care for this. In the rooms where I go, they would simply turn around and walk out. They are the ones I admire. And my Grandfather, now dead - is he looking down at me? Is he the one who speaks to me out of the Chinese Book, when some sentient being answers my questions? My Mother has told me of two instances when she was confused about what to do, and she went someplace or other - the Doctor's office in one case, the post office in the other - and someone in each place spoke to her, and in his words was each time the complete answer to her question - In both cases, the man she met was a retired former engineer, off the subways, and that was my Grandfather's job. Then she would say, "Alright, thanks, Pop, you told me what I had to know!" Yes, he is there, and he is here. We live in the world observed by family spirits. Family spirits help the living to live. This is the meaning of that strange article in the *Times*, about how those who died in the U.S. found Heaven to be a certain way, while those who had died in India found their Heaven to be entirely different. Our Heavens are the geographical homes where our family's old spirits dwell, watching over us, preparing our geographical heavens for our arrival.

But if this is so, what does my Grandfather think of me now? Am I alright in his eyes? Do you think this is OK?... He was accepting of all things, that is true. Maybe he understands that I have nothing else right now. If it weren't for the heat coursing through me, propelled by the heroin, this would be an empty room, except for a man lying on a bed, unshaven, blowing his nose, listening to the rain. It has rained for three months, everyone says. Everyone says it has rained for three months, at least three or four days a week... But years, year, this has been going on, this solitude. I don't ever like to call it by a name. Because its name is certainly solitude. And, Gramps, the people I meet, they're not made for me, I'm not made for them. I want things to go well for them, but I can't sit still with them. I have no wife. I tried to go back home, but I couldn't stay there. The girl I love is married to another man. Last night I found out her husband is broke... I was with Trace and she said something about Susan having to get up early to go to work. Trace tells me all Susan's husband's money has been spent in the vain pursuit of expensive projects. Susan is working to feed herself and her husband, while he looks for a job.

She said, "Their marriage isn't really on the rocks, but I think she's pretty pissed at him."

Now, "The Lady Came From Baltimore," is on the radio.

I can't believe it. Not another damn dawn! Even in the midst of our three months' rain! Everyone who comes to this apartment says we are lucky about trees, and it is true. There are a row of bushy trees across the street, facing our front windows, and there is a beautiful tree in the courtyard, higher than the 3rd Floor, where Marty and Joyce are. There are also a few smaller trees. Birds seem to live in all the trees, or visit them, according to their schedules.

"I don't understand," said Trace, slightly annoyed it seemed to me. "You always talk about how you wish you had married Susan, but why didn't you?"

"I wanted to be literary, and always live with the same woman, but not get married."

I ate my club sandwich, but it was like paper to me. Old scenes, and old words, are clearer to me than anything between me and a woman at any time since then. Why? Is it really true that we only love once in our entire lives. Once. It may be for a week, but we will never find anyone we love as much as the one we loved during that one week of love, and so that one, that was it for us - we may not know who it was until years after that one has left the scene, but once, once, once ... only once... What about freedom? What about our freedoms? All thc contacts we make, like bits of information, touching, bipping, bipping, swooping off to another intersection of blips...

But what if one time is all we get? Once.

"Ego!" I said to Trace, rubbing a steak fry in a pile of salt I had placed there for that purpose. "It wasn't ego! I loved her, I didn't want to lose her! Was she kidding, or what? I mean, didn't she get it?"

T. was a little shocked, I think. "I don't know, she said very softly, even for her, which meant she was angry.

I couldn't stop.

"She used to tell me all I ever thought about was myself," I said. "But it wasn't true. I was thinking about *things* - things - everything - but not myself particularly..."

I realized there was no point in telling T. all this. It was old news, from years ago; it was scenes she had not been at. "But this is horrible," I said, "just terrible. Reversals, that's what I hate the most in life - these reversals of fortune."

"Really," she said. "But what can you do?" "It's hopeless."

"When you think of the things that can happen - my god. Did I tell you about Rose? All the terrible things that have happened to her - with her health, her sons getting into trouble, one dying and she goes to church every single day and prays... Now, how can things like that happen to someone who prays every day of her life, on her knees, to God, in church?"

"Well, they pray out of necessity," she said.

I couldn't tell if that was supposed to be funny, or what. Trace is like that. She has a very dry humor, whose purity admits no imperfections in the form of sentiment.

The man on the radio has just said that 19 weekends out of the last 26, we have had rain or threats of rain.

Monday. June 4. 9:53 A.M.

Trace said the junk make her feel "very feminine" and her skin feel like velvet. She speaks of what she considers to have been her gradual masculinization, as a result of having to fight the business world. She is 27, successfully advancing in her profession, but she is tired of drawing to sell, and tired of selling. She can't remember what she had in mind when she started.

What was I thinking about?

Tues. June 5. 4:50 A.M.

Bank - no money.

T. called - She was in Brentano's on 5th Ave. today, in the Fashions section, and somebody grabbed her ankle through the lower shelf. He was lying on the floor, in the Crafts section. She said she walked away, then looked back. The man got up and walked to the other side of the store. Then he came back and looked at her again.

She offered me the use of her apt. when I want to kick junk. I said, I didn't think she'd enjoy it much if I used her place for that, but she insisted she wanted me to, she wanted to help me.

A friend of Marty's was here tonight with his Balinese wife. His name is Benjamin. The point is, he, like Marty, had to fight for the right to marry his wife. Marty spent months being refused by his wife's family; Benjamin eloped with his wife, from a small village in Bali, and they were pursued by two truckloads of villagers.

5:58 A.M.

Weds. June 6. 12:35 A.M.

This is the anniversary of D-Day. There was a show on T.V. in which General Eisenhower, now himself long dead, was shown returning to Normandy Beach with Walter Cronkite, and together they sat in an old Army jeep, on the rise overlooking the beach. It looked as though the film was made after Eisenhower had been President, he was very old in it. Marty noticed he sounded like Clark Gable. The resourcefulness, the idealism, the humility, of Eisenhower, and of our Army during that war, against such awesome and terrible opponents, whom President Eisenhower would refer to as "the feller" or "the other feller," and the graves, the crosses, where Cronkite and Eisenhower were sitting at the end of the show, the thousands of white crosses, interspersed with Jewish stars - what weeping began in the room! Marty and I tried to hide our tears. The thousands of young men beneath French soil... And Eisenhower was talking like an old farmer, or a grandfather - about his own son having graduated from West Point on the same day as the invasion - 35 years ago today - that he had commanded, and the good fortune of his son, to have had a good life, to have married a lovely girl, to have had four beautiful children, who were a joy to President Eisenhower and his wife, and then he looked at the expanse of white crosses before his eyes, and talked of all those boys "cut down in their prime," and what was most of it, *to me*, was the speech he then gave - it sounded and looked as though it may have been written. He said those boys had not died, nor been sent into battle for any thought of gain, to themselves or their nation, but to help preserve certain "systems of self-government, and human freedom."

Chief Crazy Horse's famous statement was: "My Lands are where my dead lie buried." Our dead lie buried in every land, which will be changed by the seeds of these dead, in ways unknown to the rational mind, like prayer affects the world... What will happen to Rose's son? The Judge in charge of his case has told Rose that unless she can find some kind of program for him - where he will be locked in at night - he'll have to go to prison. He's too old for one program, not retarded enough for another program, other programs turned him down because he was involved in a criminal case, other programs turned him down because his crime wasn't serious enough. The agencies Rose calls are never at their phones - some have unbelievable hours, like 11-1, Monday to Friday -

and all in all, we have all been trying, but have not been able to find that thing which the Judge demands, as the only alternative to her boy being sent to a regular prison - a full-time program, where the boy will be "cared for" (locked up) 24 hours a day... The trial is tomorrow. The lawyer will try to get another extension, but there's no way of telling if he'll get it or not. Rose's son is helpless on his own. In a real prison he will surely be harmed. He may be killed...

A beautiful model was hit on the head by a cinder block, thrown from the roof of her building by some kids, and she is dead. She was 25 years old. Her name was Manderson. There was no picture of her in the paper, but she was called "a Cheryl Ladd look-alike," by her neighbors in Queens.

1:51 A.M.

Sunday. June 10. 5:17 A.M.

I could not take this notebook to Canada, for fear of Customs reading an unfortunate word, and then searching me -

Thurs.: hid dope under the buckles of my loafers, and wrapped in a plastic bag, took plane to Toronto, where I was summoned to confer w/Brian and his two partners, for whom I am working the cartoon.

Before I left, I had talked to Susan on the phone. We talked from 2 A.M. to 8 A.M. Six great, wonderful hours! She told me that she had recently been wondering why it was that, even after all the years since she and I are not together any more, she has never felt what she called "passion" with anyone except me. She said she thought it might be due to the fact that we were so young when we were together. However, I was quick to point out that women are supposed to get more passionate, w/age. She said that was an interesting point. I said I felt the same about her, that is - felt most passion for, or whatever you call it. That phone conversation was the first really long talk we have had in seven years - like we used to have. It's the first time I've talked to anybody, except to bullshit, in seven years. She asked me to come to see her before her husband returned from L.A., where he was looking for a job. I asked if she would let me kiss her, and she said she would not, because that would be an act of adultery. I am supposed to go there today, later to visit her. I should sleep. It is already 6:20 A.M. I didn't write about that call at the time because I was too knocked out by it. After all, it was the first time Susan has not dwelled exclusively on the bad, terrible things I did to her when we were together. It was the first time she has admitted, since our separation, to the survival of any feelings for me. This caused me to let down my guard, and confide similar things to her.

I said a lot of stupid things, I said I wanted her to come live with me and manage my money. I said I would give it all to her, so as not to spend it on heroin. She said she had noticed a gray hair recently, and I found myself wishing I could see her with gray hair. Anyway - who knows? Who knows?

As a consequence of my talk w/Susan I have been infused with new life. I was able to solve all the problems of the film's outline overnight, and to read off the complete story to Brian and Patrick, his partner, the next day, and receive their praise and thanks. Brian said I was a genius, a man of true capability, a master, while Patrick said he thought we were "85% there," which means the same thing to him (that is to say - when Brian calls me a genius, he means we're 85% there)... When else but after that (partial) reconciliation with my beloved, the woman chosen for me by Heaven, would I have had the energy to approach, let alone to elegantly perform, the task of creating the story they in Toronto, all of them, have been trying to nail down for the past two months? I felt like a man of great power because I was happy. How long it has been since I felt the happiness which is infused into the body by love reciprocal, instead of the sickness blown through the cells by longing for love. Since I last lived with Susan, that is the answer.

Monday. June 11. 5:30 P.M.

"Oh sister do not
turn me away
You should not treat
me like a stranger"

Bob Dylan

Friday. June 22. 10:01 A.M.

Then I went to ____________,
No. I don't want to talk about that now.

Saturday, June 23. 1:14 A.M.

Then I went to Provincetown to see Susan. I went Sunday, June 10. It was the first time we'd seen each other in two years, and that time two years ago was just a short visit, mostly spent in the company of others.

Fool that I am, I fully expected that by now my life would have been greatly changed, and much improved by Susan's leaving her husband, and coming back to New York, to live with me. However, she has not. Does this mean all hope is gone? I would have thought so, but the *I Ching* keeps loading hope onto my shoulders, forbidding my history with Susan to end once and for all. How can I be expected to maintain my optimism about this, after what happened when I visited her?

Last night, I was talking to my father. I was telling him about my visit with Susan, and it occurred to me that it might be a good idea if *he* called her. I am proud of my father, and I thought his calling her might be some kind of advertisement for me, his son after all... Besides that, Susan and my father have always gotten along.

He did phone her, and then called me back.

He sounded mournful. "She said you have a fantasy about her," he told me. She said, "I'm afraid Michael's got a fantasy about us getting together again, and it's preventing him from establishing a relationship with anyone else."

I said, "I hope you told her she's wrong," although I don't know why I said that. In fact, I do maintain a fantasy of our getting together again, and I have no objection to her knowing about it, although I have no desire for anyone else to suspect it.

My father said, "Well, I didn't want to contradict her."

I'm afraid I lost my temper at my father, over his tone of voice. "Why are you sounding so tragic? This isn't tragic - She's just crazy!" I screamed at him.

He was perfectly understanding - He didn't even balk at my rudeness. He just said he was very tired. He wasn't sounding tragic; only tired. However, he was sounding tragic, and he had every reason to. Here his son was pining for this girl who had just told him she was completely happy being married to another man, and had long ago forgotten his son.

How could he know it was all an act?

As a matter of fact, as I heard the things she told him, I found new reasons to be optimistic about our prospects for ultimate reunion. As I said to my father, "You mean she said all this without you saying one word about me?"

That was the thing.

She was evidently taking great pains to establish a "version" - a "story" - you might even call it an "alibi" - for the Great Transgression - which was bi-partate. That is - its first part was our 6-hour phone conversation, during which she invited me to visit her - and its second part was the visit itself. Here, my father was calling about something entirely other - to get her address, so he could have an invitation sent to her - and yet she had felt the need to tell him the story of a relationship that was, by her own analysis, non-existent.

But this brings us to the visit itself, and the call that preceded it.

Susan's husband was in N.Y. this month, to look for a job. I first heard about this from Trace. According to her, Susan was annoyed with Ben for not working, and for spending his days sitting around the house, writing poetry. She said Susan had "sent" Ben to New York to find a real job.

Now, it turns out, while in the city, Ben was staying with someone named Jim, a person who always has a few friends sleeping in his apartment, and one of the other guests was another old friend of Susan's and mine, a girl named Lena. Just after Susan and I broke up, back then, when we were all still hanging around New York for our different purposes, I was seeing Lena for a while. In more recent times, she has been a primary source of information concerning the subject of Susan's marriage... To Lena I have admitted, reluctantly, I'm still hung up about Susan.

So it was that Lena called me one day and, speaking in her theatrical, charming voice, said, "Darling, you'll never guess who my *room*mate is thee days!"

"Ben!" I said, because T. had told me, there being not enough room at Jim's, that Lena and Ben were sharing a room.

She laughed slyly.

"Well, how about coming and joining us for a drink?" She said. "That would be nice, don't you think?" and again she laughed.

I didn't want to meet Susan's husband at all - and especially didn't want to see him that night. I was doing something else. I told her that. She said, "Oh, what a shame! Well, you *will* have a drink with us *some*time, though, won't you?" And again, the laugh, which I now realized was meant to be a conspiratorial chuckle. I got mad, and said, "Look, I'm sure I would like to meet Ben one day, for some reason or other, or purely by chance - I don't care - We're both writers, and like that - but I definitely *don't* want to meet him on the basis that he is married to a certain woman and one time forty centuries ago I too lived with that self-same woman. I mean, who cares? And I don't see God's name is supposed to be so goddamned hilarious about the fact that you know him and you know me, or anything about this at all!"

There followed a long period of explanatory paragraphing by her and modifying phrasing by me, ending with my missing the opportunity to go have drinks with them. The one thing I had heard about him - his asking her to sign that pre-nuptial contract, I didn't like at all. The other thing - that he turned out not to have any money - that the contract was evidently designed to save from Susan earnings he would have to earn while married to her - I liked even less. The third thing - that far from piling up a fortune, he had lost whatever he had started with - made me want to meet him, if at all, at some later date, when he was in a luckier period.

However, after yelling at Lena, and repeating the whole conversation for Marty and Joyce, Susan was much on my mind, and filling my heart all over again - and I had to call her -

I started calling her, and finally, at 2 A.M., reached her... We talked about the past, and it was fairly early in the conversation when she happened to mention that she had recently been "wondering" why it was that she had never experienced the same passion with anyone else that she had with me. This (as I have already said) was the first time in seven years that Susan has said anything of this nature to me. Until now, she has taken great care to recall only unhappy things about our relationship. Now, here in plain English, was the thing she had been trying not to say when she had referred all those times to my faults. And yes, I did allow those things to have a voice - yes, as I had not done since the day of her marriage, out of respect for *her* ethical system, which I trusted above my own instincts. I said I felt the same way. "After all these years," I said, "it's amazing. Everything relating to love, pleasure, life, survival, anything positive, is wrapped up in the image of you."

Anyway, somewhere along the line, she invited me to come and visit her, and she even said (and this has since become something of a sore point) "Come before Ben gets back."

Now she says that she added " - or *after* he gets back," But I didn't hear that. Now, she seems to be covering her trail or something. Everything she says seems designed as a response, for some imagined criticism of Susan, which Susan has managed to anticipate and, by what she says, to effectively deny without the embarrassment of having to first hear the criticism at all.

Monday. June 25. 1:10 A.M.

The other thing she's started to say - it started when I was still there with her - is that she didn't invite me to visit her at all, I invited myself. That I told *her* I was going to be in the area, and I said I'd "drop by and see her." I don't remember it that way. I remember hearing about passion, hearing about the psychiatrist she and her husband are visiting, and hearing Susan invite me to come. And this is after I had said plainly that I wished she would come back to me, so when she turns around and says, as she later did, that she "thought we could be friends but she obviously mistaken," I have to wonder *how* she thought we could be friends? Was I not honest? And this is another thing. I do love her; however, it is also true that I had absolutely resolved never to talk to her again about the question of our reunification. Before she met Ben, I had seen her in New York, after another long interval, and I asked her to marry me. She had refused, with the complete artillery of bitter memories she retained from our love affair. Once, on the phone from California, I proposed. It wasn't long after that proposal that she called me to tell me she was marrying her husband, whom she had met only a week before he proposed to her.

When she told me, I tried to dissuade her. When she told me that thing about the pre-nuptial agreement, I said, "Marry me and you can have everything I ever have. Forget half. You can have it all. I don't want any of it," but it was too late...

However, the point I'm trying to make is - that *since* her wedding, I had absolutely resolved not to talk of those things with her any more, and the fact is, I didn't. Until that conversation, and then, only allowing those sentiments' release from me after I heard from her that in all the years since we've been apart, she has not felt as much passion for any other man. Then, of course, I did speak my mind, for then I knew that what I had always suspected was true - she still loved me, and she still related to others in terms of her relationship with me. Then the fact of her being married became less important.

"Why live half a life, Susan? Yes, we've been separated for seven years - that's a long time - every day I've felt I was being punished for not holding on to you when I had the chance. But this has gone far enough! Let's reverse it! We have our whole lives ahead of us."

She didn't say anything. I took this as an indication that she was luxuriating in a fantasy life blissfully shared with me... That is why I went up there to see her.

It was a beautiful day over Provincetown as the small propeller plane flew across the sand dunes and over the forests, and set down at a small airstrip, where I stood breathing the sea air until the loudspeaker called me to the phone. Susan said she had just gotten back from the beach and was about to hop in her car and come and get me. I waited in the parking lot, thinking of the year she and I had lived in this town, where nobody lived in the winter, then. Although now, she said, quite a few people stayed all year round. She drove up in a red sports car, of the kind that looks like the owner knows how to fix it if it breaks. As soon as I saw her face through the windshield, when she was still all the way across the parking lot from me, I knew I was in trouble. For a split second she didn't even acknowledge that it was me, either with her eyes or her mouth. Finally she did drop her jaw - a noncommittal form of recognition that has the advantage of carrying with it no overtones of anything.

When I got in the car and had shoved my suitcase in the back seat, she did not look at me. Instead she held her profile resolutely in my direction. It had what seemed to be a twitch. It was as though someone were trying to push her head toward the side window and only by the strength of her neck muscles could she resist the pushing palm - that was what it looked like as she drove away from the airport and I looked at her profile. She was looking beautiful. Evidently, she knew that's what I was thinking, and the source of her muscular tensions was this knowledge that she must bear up under my admiring looking. Well, I thought, she does get this way sometimes. I thought she was too sun-tanned, and dry-looking; but the greatest change in her, I thought, was that her arms were very strong, with sinews, and made me think of the hard jobs she's had, over the past few years.

When I tried to give her a hello kiss she turned her head away. And, that was that. She had obviously gotten scared between the phone call and the visit. Several times before I left she said something like, "Now you'll tell everyone - " or "Now I'll hear you said this or that - " many times drawing out of me the promise not to tell anyone of those few incriminating sentences she had allowed to escape through her living lips - the more than rare exceptional words she had said - those words that had told of a feeling actually felt by her for many years of her real life, her only life, and yet words that were good for nothing but to deny and cross out, to outflank on the field of history, where they had made their appearance, at long last, like carrier pigeons sent out from some embattled fort - to me. Over and over I swore never to tell a word. I pretended to believe her denials, finally, because of the sadness I felt whenever she once again would tell me she was really happy.

Strange thing - by the end of the two days we had a "version," agreed-upon (without that agreement being stated) as the most graceful way out for all concerned. This was - that I had misunderstood her when we talked on the phone - misunderstood her to say she was not happy - and that I had come up to rescue her, but that I had been set straight by Susan as soon as I arrived - In fact, I didn't come because I thought she was unhappy. I came because I understood her to say she still loved me.

So what? I spent the two days jabbing a needle into my left buttock and telling her she couldn't do without me. Am I surprised she decided I was not yet trustworthy enough to throw in with for life? I am not.

They have a lovely dog named Altimeter. I saw the photo album recording their wedding. Her father looked like he was having a good time. In her two albums of photos there were two photos of me. One was taken looking down at the top of my head, at the incredibly youthful, sun-warmed bridge of my long-ago nose - And the other one is of my back, as I disappear into a gloomy forest. I would not have noticed there was a person in the photo at all, but the caption said: "Hampstead Heath - 1970 - Michael Mabius" and that led me to find myself. I remembered the day it was taken.

Tues. June 26. 2:11 A.M.

When it came time to go to bed on my first night at Susan's, I said I wanted to sleep with her. It seemed to me that her manner of sending me into the guest room was lacking in kindness, lacking in warmth. I said, "I want to sleep with you. The bed in the other room is damp and cold."

"Well you're *not* sleeping with me!" she said. "And I'm occupying this bed!"

"Why don't you sleep on the floor?" I said.

This infuriated her. I tried to explain that I was only answering her with the same tone she had been using on me. She said I was trying to get her to commit adultery. She wasn't that kind of person.

I said, "I know you're not. I don't want you to commit adultery," which was a lie, "I only want to lie next to you one more time before I die, since I've lost you forever."

As I've said, from then on the depressing period began, during which she proceeded to take back, deny, or consign to the realms of "misunderstanding" all the honest things she had told me over the phone.

I argued as long as my optimism held out, but ultimately the weight of her dishonesty crushed me down. I said, "Well, I came here because it sounded like you'd finally decided to admit to yourself you've never gotten over me, and I was going to *save* you, bring you back to New York with me, let you manage all the money I make. And you would help me get off dope - but now I feel, I mean - what am I *doing* here?"

"It was all a misunderstanding," she said. "I'm very happy. My husband loves me. Very much. We have problems, but we're working them out. We see a psychologist twice a week to work out our problems. Does that sound like two people who don't love each other?" she asked. I said it sounded like one did, one didn't.

I went to sleep in the guest room. I spent most of the night shooting dope and asking the *I Ching* how the fuck it had advised me to go up there. "I didn't need this humiliation" I told it. At one point, of course, I became so angry I started tearing the book to shreds. After all - this was a landmark in my life's disappointments. But I did it very quietly, so as not to wake Susan.

The next day, I awoke at 5 P.M., an hour after the last plane left the island for the day. I now ask myself, why didn't she wake me in time to get that plane?

That second night there we did sleep together, but nothing happened.

She was disappointed in me. I'm sure of it. I failed her. Now - will she ever come back to me?

I may be crazy, but I think she will.

She said, "Do you think I still love you because we had one friendly phone conversation?" I said, "No - I think you still love me because of all the lousy phone conversations we've had."

I left on the third day - without her. She drove me to the airport. The day was blue and cold. She reassured me that she was happy. I said I was glad to hear it. We kissed. I walked into the terminal building alone, turning, smiling, waving...

Now why is it that as I flew off, in the little six-passenger plane, I felt *guilty*? Why did I feel I had let her down, once again?

All I had gotten from her had been rejection, but I still thought I had failed her.

Naturally, I thought, she couldn't do anything to encourage me, because that would have meant leaving her husband and living with me. Now, maybe she would have done that - maybe it was what she was thinking of before I got there - just as I had thought it was - but then, when I arrived, she saw how heavily dependent on the heroin I was, and she realized that I would offer her nothing at all in the way of security.

Well then - why had I made such an open display of the needle?

Yes, I must have known I had to appear a certain way if she were going to commit herself to such a radical move - but I showed up as the opposite of what was called for in that situation...

She snorted a small amount of junk, but wouldn't shoot it. She gave me disapproving looks as I cooked the spoon, filled the syringe, etc.

What a fool!

To what a fumbled form of courtship did I entrust my future happiness!

Now Susan seems to be covering her tracks, fashioning her alibis.

I can tell from what she said to my father. She's got her version of the "incident" down pat.

Really, she had nothing to worry about from me.

As I stepped in the door, back from the flight, the phone was ringing. It was Trace - Susan's old friend - sounding angry.

"You didn't tell me you were going to see Susan!" she said in an accusatory tone. "What did you go there for?"

"How did you find out?"

I knew she and Susan don't talk that often.

"Ben called and told me."

"Was he upset?"

"Well - he said that intellectually he could understand it, but emotionally it bothered him slightly."

"It did?"

"Mm. He said, 'Here am I in New York, trying to get a job, to get things together, because she asked me to, and she's having her old boyfriend visit her while I'm away.'"

"What did you say?"

"Well - I told him you and Susan were friends - that you still care about one another, what happens to one another - but it's nothing for him to worry about... I mean, I don't know if I was right or not, but it seemed like the thing to say."

"Right. It was. If you talk to him again, tell him you asked me, and it was just a friendly visit."

"OK."

"Are you fucking Ben?"

"No!" - pause - "What made you ask that?"

"Just a thought."

"Well, what happened? How was it up there?"

"It was very nice seeing Susan. You know - nice house, nice dog. I thought she wasn't happy, but I guess she is."

I didn't tell her anything much.

She said, "Did you mention anything about us?"

"Not a word," I said, "and I'd appreciate it if you'd never say anything about it either. OK?"

"Oh, sure. I had no intentions of saying anything to anyone."

She wanted to see me that night but I didn't feel like it, and I haven't seen her or talked to her since then. That was about a week ago.

I feel like being alone for a while. Re-grouping. Figuring things out. What am I doing? What do I want? I thought I wanted Susan, and I do, but even with all the years of desire, even knowing that I've never found any woman who means half as much to me as she does - Still, there's no denying the fact that when I left there, alone, I was somewhat relieved.

Relieved?

To be alone, still. To have no responsibilities. I was content to know she was safe and secure, in her home, and I was content to be alone.

However - and here is the pinnacle of all the madness and pigheadedness contained within me at this time - I now felt more strongly than ever that we *would* be together again - that we *would* ultimately marry.

I had not failed to notice that on the subject of children she was still as definite as she had been when first considering the idea of marrying this man - She was definite in not wanting them.

Now it is 4:04 A.M. I was recently 31 years old. Last year there were 200 people at a party to celebrate my birthday. This year I'm sure not one of those people realized that day's anniversary had come around again. There were three cakes at the party last year. One of them was sat in by an actress who writhed in it on the floor. The next morning, someone was found in the flower patch behind the building, lying there in a walking position, like a figure walking around the face of a Greek vase. Broken whiskey bottles. Strange visitors. Large garbage bags. It was all right, but I couldn't stand it.

I managed to get away to the Seven-11 Store on La Cienega for about an hour, where I read the Western Magazines... "He stands to protect me from danger/When all my earthly friends are gone/He promised never to leave me/ Alone... He promised (Yes he did) never to leave me, never to leave me alone, No, never alone, no, never alone, He promised never to leave me, Never to leave me alone..." "The very dedicated Dixie Hummingbirds."

"Two youths in New Jersey found out that crime does not pay... While stealing a bicycle lock one of the boys was arrested... The other boy ran from the store ... but ... he didn't get far... When he got outside of the store ... he found that both his and his friend's bicycles had been stolen..."

"A teenage girl struck by falling concrete while walking past Gimbel's Department Store... She is recovering... She is reported to be a 15-year old girl, who is both deaf and dumb. She cannot hear, or speak."

Incredible! That's the fourth story of someone being hit by falling stones, pieces of concrete or brick in the last month! How can this be? There was a girl near Barnard, the model in Queens, that other incident, and now this - why?

"He's been a shelter for me, a shelter for me, He's been a shelter for me, he sure has been a shelter for me, he's been a shelter for me..."

But what is going on with these falling stones? "You ought to meet the Lord, Before you come to die. You're going to need the Lord, Before you come to die."

"I gave it all up for the Lord... I gave it all up for the Lord... Talk about the point of no return - The Lord knows that I've been by..."

I listen to the gospel station, and think of Susan some more.

Weds. June 27. 3:47 A.M.

I feel like a character in a primitive religious ritual. Wherever I touch myself, I spurt blood. I refer to the needle. I never shoot for the vein, because I'm a coward. Usually, where I shoot, there's no blood, but today and yesterday, for some reason, the point seems merely to touch my skin and deep red blood pours out. Naturally, this has been attracting mosquitoes. One day soon I will stop taking drugs altogether.

I can't stand it any more. You're always wondering if you feel good or not, you must feel good because god you've tried so hard to feel good, you've spent so much money, you've sacrificed so much self-esteem, you'd better at least feel absolutely magnificent! Glazed! But you soon discover that most of the time you are experiencing exactly the same range of happiness and sadness, and the same range of calm and excitement, that everyone else on earth is experiencing. The only way to reproduce the euphoria, warmth, release, or whatever you want to call it, of the first time, you have to allow the stuff to completely leave your system, which means you must undergo a certain amount of discomfort. The problem with me is that I dread the slightest discomfort, so I never take the few days required to re-establish the body's original function for a while, before knocking it to pieces again. Tom is always either very stoned or suffering the agonies of withdrawal. I on the other hand, have opted for a steady drone of peace, a pharmacological security. I once staggered in and had my blood pressure tested in a health food store on Hollywood Blvd. and the man said I had the lowest blood pressure he'd ever tested. He said that was very good. However, he did ask me if I was taking aspirin at the time.

My fear of pain. Therefore, all the more reason to fear, now that I notice I will soon be out of dope. What's more - I'm broke. I've spent $48,000 on junk in the last 2 years, and that money is gone. My last buy was a full gram, which I got because I thought I would use it to withdraw, scientifically. Instead, I have squandered it, like much else... Like much else, and many other, it is gone... What to do next?

It just occurred to me - if Susan were to call me right now and say she wanted to come back to me, I wouldn't be able to support her. I wouldn't even be able to send her a ticket. The very thing I was trying to sell her on - my new identity as a provider, my maturity as reflected in success - that very thing is once again, as it was when she loved me, my weakest suit.

Maybe she wouldn't care. But still - the thought of having to explain, after I bragged about all the money I made - I couldn't face it - So now. What if she does call, and says she's been thinking about it, and I'm right, we can't go on apart - what will I do? She'll sense my hesitation - should I simply admit what I've done. No. She'll never come back to me then. Or will she? Do I confuse her with someone else? Susan has never cared about my money. No, but she married a rich man. Yes, but... But I can just see me, with my head hung down (to hide a smile), saying, "Baby, I'm sorry, I lied when I said I was loaded. I'm broke. Yes, I meant it when I said you would manage all my money to prevent me from spending it on heroin, but you got here too late..."

And she'd say, "I knew it!" and laugh, and hug me and kiss me with her sweet, memorious lips, and say, "I love you, with or without money."

I've been trying to be strong when I really want to be weak, and not only that - everyone would prefer it if I were weak.

It is, they claim, 88 degrees now... I put on the heat anyway. I wonder if something dangerous happens if you turn on this electric heat in the summertime. I was amazed it worked at all, but it did... It goes click click click, and then the heat comes up. But it wasn't enough to warm me. My back is freezing. I slid across the bed under the covers, until my back was pressed right up against the heater. Finally, I felt *just* warm enough. But I had to pull myself away when I smelled my flesh burning. It smelled like a rubber tire burning. Then I lay there 2 inches from the heater, until a feeling of sharp needles started to saw throughout my inward parts, in a pattern of twin radiations. I think I will now have blisters on my spine, but it couldn't be helped...

Thursday the Twenty Eighth of June at one a.m.

Marty smells trouble. He is worrying about the rent money. He told me this morning, as he sat in my living room on the rattan love seat loaned to us by his mother, as I sat in a rattan chair, drinking coffee and gazing out at the workers in the Salvation Army, who were just getting ready to go to lunch... Marty overheard me telling someone on the phone that Brian has refused to advance me any more money. He pointed out that I was already a month late with the rent, and that the next rent is due in less than two weeks... I tried to comfort him by sharing with him the knowledge that Brian will pay me a few grand when I finish the mouse script.

Marty sat there twirling his beard. I hate talking about money with him. He's one of those people who *al*ways offers you money the moment you've just told him you don't need it, and who *never* offers you money if there is the slightest possibility you might have any use for it. This way, he manages to bathe himself in feelings of generosity almost all the time, interrupted only by those few, unavoidable moments when he comes across someone who actually is short of money. He gets over these rough spots by beating the needy one to the draw, so to speak, and giving forth with a list of his upcoming bills, and his most recent financial setbacks. This he did to me, after a short stretch of glaring at me as I gazed out the window, glaring and twisting the central point of his beard, back and forth, until it seemed the beard would be pulled out of his chin from the twisting. "That's great about Brian," he said, "because the store is really doing shitty, really shitty ... and I told you about the new gates we had to put, didn't I? And the new sprinkler system?"

"Sure, Marty, it'll be all right, don't worry."

Marty doesn't know about my involvement with junk... Like many political radicals he is very conservative on this one question. I have often heard him speak with great horror, great contempt, about friends who have succumbed to dope. I do not have the optimism or the spunk to tell him the truth about my own situation. I don't want to argue with him about it, or hear what he has to say about it, or have that feeling I always get when I'm around someone who's trying to improve me.

The result of my keeping this secret from him, which I started to do without really thinking about it, just to avoid embarrassment, is that there is now a huge cloud over our friendship - the secret - and this has distanced me from him, in my own mind, and made me treat him with less consideration, in various ways, than he deserves. I don't want to hear his perceptions, I don't want to hear him praising himself - I have no intention of being honest with him, if I can help it.

Thurs. June 28. 4:05 A.M.

Nine boxes of my papers, notebooks, scripts, letters and photographic memories arrived today from my father. I had sent them to his place, because I thought I would be living with him after I left L.A. What ever happened to that idea? Anyway, here they are. I was ultimately blocked from going through them any more because everywhere I looked there were pictures of Susan and letters from Susan. Finally I said "Give me a break," and left them. There she was in England, there she was in Algeria, sitting on the lawn of that hotel, with her hair wet from the shower, there she was on the cover of "Deathburger," and so on. What a beautiful girl. Is there still hope? I was not going to think about her, but now these photos are before me - And this gigantic pile of letters, all from her. Here - she's written me on my birthday every single year - how come she pretended not to remember when it was, when I saw her? I suppose using my own criteria for optimism - that is - that all displays of disinterest, on her part, are actually evidence of continued love - I should be jumping for joy. You don't remember someone's birthday for 15 years and then forget it suddenly. Or is that an effect of her domestic bliss? I shouldn't talk this way. I do wish her happiness, nothing but happiness - I only believe she is denying any hope of happiness for either one of us by her actions - When I was up there I said, "I know, I realize I did every terrible thing possible, but I also realize you could have forgiven me. My sins had everything except forgiveness." She said she forgave me when she was in Latin America.

"That's a great place to forgive anyone," I think I said. Oh, Susan, I'm looking at a picture of you, exactly what I had decided not to do.

When I was up there I made a confession to her, that one time, a few years ago, after I had seen her in New York, and we had spent a few days together during which she was exceedingly bitchy, I went back to L.A. and the next week, called her from there. I told her about a girl I had met - 17 years old. I was in love - we were going to the desert together, to a place called Joshuatree - and I told Susan how lovely the place was, how lovely the girl was - what I confessed was that this had all been a lie. There was no such girl. She gave me the sweetest smile when I confessed that - as though she were thoroughly enchanted by me - it was a brief sensation.

Friday. June 29. 2:54 A.M.

What's in the news today? A hundred thousand "boat people" - Viet Namese citizens, expelled from their homeland by their government. No nation wants them. Malaysia repulses them with guns. The U.S. takes 7,000 a month, but that's not many. It is estimated that 65,000 per month are drowning. Just now, Marty was screaming about what the U.S. should do to save these people. Everything he said, I had been thinking, earlier in the day - but it got on my nerves hearing him shout about it, because I could see he was just having fun. It is fun to be morally outraged. I told him to call up the State Department and offer to sponsor a Viet Namese family, and then he would have saved at least one family. Why don't I do that? No, I have to buy heroin so I can stick it in my legs and write dialog for rats to say as they're chasing each other around in the post-nuclear-holocaust landscape. Now I'm just back from kissing that picture of Susan, which fell out from between the pages. It's a nice, cool night. I haven't slept for about 80 hours. Why? Did I tell you how she saved my life?

It's too late to call her, or I'd call her right now and remind her of that. Doesn't she owe me something, having saved my life. Is she really being fair? Perhaps I was supposed to die then, and by saving me then she was taking responsibility for my life.

4:35 A.M.

T. called tonight. She was surprised when I cut short the recitation of her adventures, with the question, "Have you talked to Susan recently?" Surprised in part because she hardly ever talks to Susan. However, it was all I wanted to know at that time. Then I said, "I have to go back to the T.V., can I call you Monday? Is it OK? Thanks for calling..." and other exit lines. I was watching *Quincy*, a show about a race car driver who is poisoned by amphetamines injected into an orange. Someone knew he was going to eat it before the last lap of the race. The Coca Cola ads for the summer are extremely sexy. This new one tonight starts with a close-up of a big round bikini-covered breast, and the place where it lays against the tan ribcage of the girl, who then waves at a speedboat.

4:56.

I just looked out on 15th Street and saw a young doctor and nurse going off to work at St. Vincent's Hospital. They were both dressed all in white. Even their socks, or stockings, and shoes. They were both younger than I am. They looked very serious, they were sleepy. They were going off to the emergencies of 5 A.M. at St. Vincent's, which is a tough hospital. I saw a man there once, in the emergency ward, lying on a table, with a knife sticking out of his chest. I hope they don't get anything like that. I am one of those men who love nurses, just for being nurses, and hate doctors, just for being that.

Sat. June 30. 1:45 A.M.

T. called when I was out to ask if I wanted to go to Connecticut w/her for the week-end. Very kind. Maybe she likes me more than it seems. Sort this out. Of course, I won't do it, but I probably should. I have been terribly rude these past three days, especially to Marty. Whenever he wants to talk to me, I have to run away. Even I have no idea why this is so. Usually, I love to listen to him talk - about his store, his family, the guilt of the United States for everything happening in the world - (to which I generally reply, "Marty, we're just another underdeveloped country, like everybody else.") - but these days, along with hollow eyes and cheeks, I am developing a perverse love for solitude and quiet - or only the sounds of motors, near and far, and of engines passing by - All the more strange, since - as I now recall - all day I have been visited in my mind by ideas of things to buy for Marty and for his wife to show my affection. What I finally did buy was some sliced ham and cheese, a cake, and a quart of ice cream. However, throughout the day I had been thinking of certain books I want to get him; after-shave lotion from the Waldorf Astoria, a table and chair for him to type on; it always seems to happen this way with me: exactly those people about whom I have the most fond, and most generous, feelings, when I am alone, these are exactly the people I act least kindly toward, when I am with them - as though to balance all the love and attention I have showered upon them in their absence, with equal amounts of rudeness and disinterest, when they are actually with me.

How often have I wished to express my love for my brother, and my admiration for him - only to miss saying anything at all! And all the years of separation - these are becoming a life of their own - a horrible growth of vines - all the years we have all been separate from one another - he and I, our mother, our father, our Grandfather - lonely satellites -

The point is - he was in town this week. I saw him - we had a chance to speak - but that opportunity to be happy was lost because of me -

Because I know he could use some money - He is teaching, and the pay is terrible. He has just split up with his girlfriend, so he has to pay twice as much rent, and so on - But I had no money to offer him, because I've squandered it all on dope - consequently, I was angry at *him*. Not that he asked for any money - but I wanted to give him some and he needs it, and I don't have it, and I can't even mention it to him. I can't explain where my money has gone. I made the mistake, as I always do, of telling the whole family exactly how much I was being paid for the script I'm writing. On the subway, where we sat together on our way downtown, I could hardly look him in the eye. I acted nerve-wracked. This was because of my well-deserved shame at not living up to my responsibilities. I must have looked as though I was in intense pain. When he shook my hand, before he got off at 59th Street, he looked at me strangely.

Tues. July 3. 5:49 A.M.

Jack, I have decided to send you these notes. I have been thinking about you more and more often. I'm thinking of the long talks we used to have. All day you would barely say a word, just listen, listen to everyone - but at night you would make yourself a cup of tea, and start spinning out endless strands of knowledge and poetic diatribe. If only I could ask you for the answers, the answers to that which is no topic. But then, even look at what has happened to you. Yes, I know you told me about the manuscript you were half done with, but a girl lost it, and I remind you that girl was long ago, and that manuscript was 10 years ago. The world is full of people like you and me - who saw what had to be done, and were certainly meaning to do it.

Now It's 6:43 A.M.

I can't sleep. What's the sense of trying to normalize my hours? I lie here trying to find a way into the world of sleep by curling myself up as tight as possible, to fit through the bottle-neck that separates me from unconsciousness.

Ah, there it is. The song. *"You can turn the world on with a smile/ You can take a nothing day and suddenly make it all seem worthwhile..."* I told Marty I thought the character Mary Richards, played by Mary Tyler Moore, had many qualities that remind you of Jesus' mother, the Virgin Mary. Even the song, I said, had religious overtones - He said I was crazy - I said I thought WJM-TV stands for "Was Jesus' Mother-The Virgin." Then there's also the way she is - the way she helps everyone else with their problems. And there's her solitude, without a husband, and various other things too embarrassing to mention. Were these things the intention of the people who made the show, or were they a sort of "spiritual intention" intended by spiritual beings, or forces, as a gift to people who, like myself, find ourselves awake at 2 in the morning every morning...

Then, last week, I was in Washington Square Park, buying grass and a man whom I had seen there before, came over and steered me away from one dealer, and toward another. Afterward, I went over to thank him. He said he was a musician, and he wrote music. He is the writer - as it turned out - of the theme song of *The Mary Tyler Moore Show*. I forgot, at the time, all my theories about Mary Richards. I felt very lucky to meet him, and be able to talk to him - I asked if he had always wanted to be a musician. He said no, he had started out to be a minister. He was thrown out of Bible College. When I asked him why, he said, "It was for a thing you probably never heard of."

I said, "What was that?"

"It's called mariolatry," he said.

When I saw Marty and Joyce, I told them triumphantly that I had been *right* about *The Mary Tyler Moore Show*, and the proof was that I had met the author of the theme song, and he had been expelled from school for mariolatry. Since that day, Marty and Joyce have kept their distance.

Who can blame them?

Which brings me to the subject of my much-considered suicide...

I won't do it. I want to hang around for a while longer. However, I did buy a gun last week. You'll be interested in this. It's a .38 caliber police special. That is the name by which the man who sold it to me kept referring to it. He's a junk-taker I met at my friend's house. He had taken the gun from his father - a policeman - when he left his home in Michigan, and he needed the money. It wasn't expensive. I will admit I had a short time there, when I would take the gun out, look at it, roll it around, put it on the bed - but then I decided to calm down. I do believe one can control oneself. One is capable of willing *peace*, in the most bloody internal wars. I'm going to sell it as soon as I can, or break it to pieces and throw it out.

I'm sure I'll recover from this time. I'll find a woman to take my mind off of Susan. (Although, I'm sure you must remember I was always easily confused when it came to her, even back then).

End of Book IV.

Book V

And I have also decided about the dope situation. That is to say, if more money gets here in time, and I think I need it - I'll buy more - but only in order to work - to finish the screenplay about my friends the Rats, because I don't want to let Brian down - And likewise, if money (and therefore, dope) doesn't get here - I'll assume the responsibility for my own dilemma - since there is certainly no else to blame - and will accept the pain, the psychological miseries, and crawling skin. I've done it before. Of course, I could kick myself to think that I was all through with this crap, once and for all, but I put myself back on it again for the purpose of instilling warmth and wit into yet another screenplay, with yet another set of barriers that almost assure it will never see the light of day. You get to a point in any case where you say "Great!" "Good!" "I deserve it!" as your bones ache and your flesh burns, and your eyes itch & freeze, and so on - You finally get to where you are sick of avoiding pain and you throw yourself into the pain with your whole heart. I've done it before. It was eight days before I could put on a shirt without feeling like the shirt was made of wet sand. I am not only ready to go through a complete withdrawal, I crave it! I welcome all attendant pains as though they were cardinals come to a cardinals' conflagration and I were their Holy Site of Red. Then, after I have regained control of my physical self, mastered my addiction, become the beloved cousin of pain, I will start on a new project, about which I have not yet had a chance to tell you, but I will now - I have the desire building in me to do something with no tendrils of the past attached to it, no arteries connected to any tradition at all, and with no debts to the dead - It's what I was thinking of, what I dimly had in my brain when I was twelve, and arguing with my father about the kind of books I would one day write. Now, penniless (as I will probably be in a few days) - I shall create my form!

I already have a name for it - "The Autobiograph." There are specific rules to the construction of an Autobiograph, these rules being necessary in order for the form to answer all the needs which it is designed to answer.

The first necessity is that it be written all in one sitting, in the presence of other people - not ever, not ever, in solitude. The plan is for Autobiographs to be written in public places. In places where you can see your fellow man and woman walking back and forth, eating, talking, playing chess - it doesn't matter what. The first ones I did were at the airport in L.A. That's when it started. I had to get out of my room. I thought of all the world's writing, and all of it having been done *in solitude.* There must be some strength to be derived from the presence of humans, just as there is an undeniable power to be drawn from their absence - and this *new* kind of power was just the type that was now needed, and that was where I went, - to the Airport - and sat on chairs in the areas where people were waiting for others to come in, or were waiting themselves to take off on one of the flights, and where the people who were arriving in the city were sure to pass by me, and there I stayed, writing. After several hours, it happened that I attracted the attention of the security guards of the airport, and two men asked me what I was waiting for. I told them what I was doing, the Autobiographs, and they both allowed crooked grins to pierce their facial armoring, and after that would greet me kindly every day, and I saw them point me out to three other men one time who seemed to be visiting dignitaries of the Security field. It also happened that the maintenance men let me use one of the offices to smoke grass in, so I could do that, and then throw myself into the maelstrom of the public lounge during some multiple-arrival, which was the kind of occasion that would set me to writing at a furious pace, frantically trying to keep up, in order to satisfy the Second Requirement of the Genre, that being -

To combine an *exact description* of the people who are there, with a description of the writer's internal workings - his feelings, thoughts, and the occasions for them, which will necessarily include memories.

In other words, the idea of the Autobiograph is to attack some element of your life passionately, while at the same time, in counterpoint, reacting to the portraits of mankind thrown at you by chance & nature as you write.

The people around you, by their presence, their availability for study and observation, and through whatever feelings or energies do cross between the skins of strangers as they come in physical proximity to one another - as well as what they say to you, or one another - all these things help you learn about that *other* thing you're writing about, at that very moment - that old love affair, that girl you've lost forever, or whatever else you have on your mind.

It is not autobiography because the goal is different. As much as possible, the events told in each autobiograph should *not* be understood by me as I transcribe them... And it shall be, as by decree, that no autobiograph shall concern itself with only one person - the author, or any other subject, alone - But the writer *and* the interactive object - passing and ever present - make the Autobiograph...

The first results were good. I had been right about the power of the life-energies of nearby people. I found that once I was ready, that is, geared up for the continuous exertion that would result from this form of working, incredible insights seemed to be borne forth toward my brain pan, and onto my pages, out of the brains of the thousands and thousands who were by me, in the many directions. Also, there was the added benefit of the epic sense of things you get merely from looking up, and looking again, at face after face after face, at hands, legs, coats, at family groups, at girls, men alone, workers at their jobs, at faces searching, at eyes reading, eyes crying, or looking, while avoiding interlocking looking which is the constant occupation of our eyes in these days, and so on - I would be trying to figure something out about my childhood (an example I happen to remember right now) only to look up from my papers, and see the answer on the faces of two nuns buying a newspaper.

Why is this?

My own theory, based only on the feelings that have swarmed through me is that the world *means* to tell us something. I think it wants to tell us things all the time, really, just about every second, it's *try*ing to tell you one thing or another. However, you might say all science is based on the assumption that the world is *not* trying to tell us anything, because if it assumed the Universe were actively attempting to convey some message, that message would instantly become suspect.

However, in the random chain of passing faces you can find the re-enactment of every relationship you've ever had, you can see everything you ever feared or hoped for - and the writing is a way to catch it, to take down the dictation coming from beyond yourself.

The other thing autobiographs would achieve would be to put writers into the world, on a daily basis, where they could be seen by fellow citizens, who should see writers, say - "There is a writer - " and know he's attempting to receive signals from them - "Let's talk to him," they might say, on seeing some furiously scribbling author somewhere. And they might report their most important things, to be included in the story of their time and place... I realize how silly this sounds. But still, give it the benefit of the doubt, because - think of the benefits - Although it is over and over reminded to us that we each go through life alone, we are also doing it together... I have to find the autobiographs I wrote down at that airport and send them to you. Anyway, that's what I'll do when out of work...

Tom said he heard from a couple of people in L.A. I'm strung out. He tried to convince them it wasn't true, but they giggled slyly. I suppose this means I won't be getting any more script jobs, which is fine with me. It was like writing with invisible ink. Five years, six years... The work disappeared faster than the money I was paid. Down the holes of vast potential, I found no way of having my writing carried to the light. I thought, Noone will ever know what I had wanted to say. I began to compensate myself for the suffocation of my words by living a fool's life. It was as though you wrote a letter to someone you loved, and gave it to a messenger to deliver, and the messenger put it in his drawer, and every year took it off his income taxes. The messenger calls you in to tell you what he liked and disliked about your message. You say, "Well, give it to the one for whom it was intended - she'll understand!" But the messenger says, "I know what she'll understand better than you, because I've taken messages to her hundreds of times. Yours won't get any response." Then you go out in the dazzling world of society, taking a rest from your mole-like existence, and there you see the messenger, telling everyone he wrote your letter. I must sleep.

WRITTEN IN THE PARK.

I looked up and it was day. I think I slept 2 hours. I washed my face and walked over to here. On the way I remarked to myself that it was a clear, cool morning, and I saw several young ballerinas going to class, all with their hair rolled into buns at the back of their heads. All with crane-like spinal/neck extensivities. They stepped carefully past the branch library on 6th Avenue, where a tramp was sleeping in a niche, or nave, in the wall, that looked like it had once been a water fountain. His feet were hanging out into the street, and his head was at such an angle against the wall of the building, that it looked like his neck was broken. The lovely, straight girls turned around to look at the face of the man. It was as though the bright threads in a rug's pattern, as they coursed through the width of the pattern, passed a muddy grey, broken-off thread, one whose time of passing through threads was done, and these gold threads were able to feel sorrow for the other, as well as for themselves, on seeing the other. It was almost that abstract, because the girls were totally new, and he was not at all new. He could have been dropped on to their bright path from an airplane, without a parachute.

It is a grey, brisk dawning in Washington Square Park.

Old men are picking through the trash bins - close, far, and in the middle distance. They are bending over - none of them allow any of the trash to fall out of the bins - if some does, they put it back, unlike in some foreign countries. The men who slept in the park last night are just now waking up... One fat man, who is black, sleeps with his profile in the lap of his friend, a white man with a bowl haircut, also pudgy jowled. Another black man, in a jeans jacket and dungaree-hat stumbles through the grass shouting, "Fuck New Yawk! That's how I feel, anyway! Fuck New Yawk!" He stumbles into the center of a group of Spanish kids who are playing with a little white dog who is jumping up and down among their arms... They react in a sophisticated manner, they disappear... Nearby, an ugly man of about 25, blonde, wearing a T-shirt, covered with yellow dirt, as though he had just come from crawling through the sun, drinks from a huge brown bottle of beer. I see by the digital watch whose band is stretched around his white elbow that it is 7 AM. A black man walks by with basketball sneakers and a clerical collar showing through under his windbreaker. Suddenly, the sound of tumbling bottles, clattering in a can somewhere... "Do he bite? Do he bite if he a smart dog?" said a voice from somewhere. Suddenly the voice was right in front of me, saying, "You need a light you need a light if you a smart boy." He has noticed the unlit cigarette hanging from my lip. Many *young* bums, *young* drunks ... "The New Drunks" ... are in the park this morning. They all sound lively, too. It doesn't seem they've had a very bad night. Always keep the option of bum-hood open. There are always parks, and other bums for neighbors... Meanwhile, a group that might be called The Circularly Mobile are running in circles around the park, so that it is almost possible to think of the joggers as engaging in a ritual conquest of the forces contained in the park - They jog to defeat the degenerate, roofless mode, represented by the tramps who occupy the center of the circle which the joggers form. The joggers are mostly students and faculty of NYU, and all the buildings facing the park belong to NYU.

Suddenly I hear the words - "My sister!" and 20 young girls, all plump, all in white blouses are running across the squares of grass, to see one girl punch another one to the ground and kick her repeatedly...

(Pause)

Now, I too have run over here... The police are here. They turned the siren on for less than a second. All the girls drifted away.

Now an old man with a white beard, a cane, white sneakers, a yachtsman's cap and the sleeves of his jacket coming down no further than his elbows has come hobbling down the lane and has stopped right in front of me. He says...

"She was kicking the shit out of that girl!" He pauses. He totters precariously as he turns his head to face me full on. He says, "I missed the shit out of it!" and looks at me as he appears to be falling sideways, even after I have said, "She sure did. You sure did." in response.

Here come the same runners I saw from the other bench. What took them so long? One is a beautiful, small girl with two blonde pigtails bouncing on her shoulders... Meanwhile, the young tramps go by at a stately pace, since they are not yet high. I just saw the one I saw before, on the way here, sleeping in a niche in a wall of the library on 6th Avenue... What has caused him to stagger here to this place? Companionship? A guy with a female wig just stopped to ask if I was doing my writing on a dictionary. I showed him it was the Oxford edition of "Selected English Essays," and he said: "Oh, is Bacon in there?" in a very gay voice. He had a pencil sticking through the black wig. He is black himself, skinny, big-eyed, wearing a red caftan. I said, "Yes, Bacon is in here." He said, "Do you know, he said, 'Books are to be swallowed, eaten, and completely digested,' in his time? Oh, he's my favorite writer. That's in *On Reading*."

I said "That might be in here." He was already down the road, calling back over his shoulder, "Read it if you get the chance."

Then a little white-haired old white lady came by opening an umbrella, for no apparent reason, and gave me a wink.

Look around! Everyone sleeps and wakes up again. Yes, some of them look insane, but somehow they manage to feed themselves, clothe themselves, and find places to sleep.

As for happiness, many people miss that in life. I consider myself lucky in that it was I, myself, who was given the privilege of thrusting my happiness from me with both hands.

It was no calumniating, no conspiring, or no blast of fate that went to make my unhappy state - It was myself, as a free man, and a cause of sorrow to those who loved me, who did it all. Everywhere I see my own work, my own dreams come true. When I was a kid I used to think of losses so vast only true heroism could bear them. The only difference between the present time, and those dreams, is that in the dreams I was a hero, and did bear these sorrows, which, as they have re-visited me in life, have not been so easy to survive, as in the pleasantly tragic dreams I used to have.

Tuesday. July 3. NIGHT.

I went to sleep around 9 A.M. An hour after the day got stale. Rose woke me at about 3 in the afternoon to clean my room. As I made my coffee, I think I remember feeling good. I felt I had come to a positive solution to my condition, and that I would soon be on the right track. Not until she was leaving did I call out, "How is it going with your son?" Her answer changed everything.

"Last night, they took him to the prison." she said. "The Brooklyn House of Detention."

"Oh, no." I said. The last I heard of it, he had been accepted into the one program in the city that fulfilled the Judge's requirements - It took Rose and the court-appointed lawyer a month just to locate this one program. However, Rose's son went into a panic there, because everyone else spoke Spanish. So, he was put into the Brooklyn House of Detention, a full-scale prison holding the worst killers, rapists and muggers. It is the kind of place where a boy like hers, who has never crossed the street by himself, should never be sent... She said, "Well, now I'm just praying every day I don't receive word that he's been killed in that place."

I couldn't believe it had happened. That in this entire city, with its hundreds of Agencies, Boards, Authorities, Councils, Bureaus and so on, there is no place at all except prison for a retarded boy who has done nothing except stand on the street with a gun in a brown paper bag (his offense) - and that now the chances are very good he will be assaulted by the guards or inmates there and be injured, or possibly die. It's as though he had fallen through the arms of mankind into hell. None of Martin's efforts, or the pleading of the lawyer that he got to work with the one appointed by the court, was able to do any good, either. He is there right now, in his cell. We have been watching this day approaching for a month now - like watching a car wreck so slow it seems it must somehow be averted, and yet is not averted.

All those sorrows which I had recently come to terms with, were, in the light of what Rose told me about her son, instantly revealed as the most debased forms of striving. Why had I bothered to come to terms with them, instead of parting with them cordially through suicide? Only so that I would be free to continue to strive. This city is full of strivers striving, yet has no place in it, where a retarded man might live and flourish, but only has a dark cell for him. After Rose left I walked around in circles. Around and around. I felt I couldn't breathe. I started imagining I was her son, in a cell, unable to comprehend, scared, listening to noises...

Now it is several hours later. Almost an entire day. The sun is coming up. Trace called before and told me her schedule is now the same as mine. She sees the dawn and then goes to sleep. She said something about hope, or something, and I said, "I need a vacation from hope," or "I'm on a vacation from hope." I didn't tell her about Rose's son, because I was afraid that if she did not react in a way that satisfied my sense of the tragedy of this incident, I would lose my temper.

What time is it?

5:52 A.M.

This is the 4th of July.

Rain is apologetically predicted.

MICHAEL'S NOTEBOOKS END HERE.

So ends the fifth and last notebook of Michael Mabius. What follows is the record of events for the last day of his life, as complete as I have been able to learn it. Keep in mind as you read, that by this time, in fact throughout the month of June and July, he was deeply and painfully subject to the power of the addiction that had already taken almost all of his money. I estimate he was taking from 1/2 to 1 gram per day of heroin. Do I say this in order to explain, or excuse, Michael's actions? Yes, I do. The increasing shame he felt, and the physical effects of that much heroin - these were the left and right hands strangling Michael during his final time on earth.

After he heard the sad news (about Rose's son) he closed the door of his room and was silent for several hours, possibly sleeping. Marty has said they had a conversation about the treatment for the cartoon Michael was writing for Brian, and after that, Marty first saw him in the early afternoon, emerging from the closed room, and he told me Michael was in a state of extreme, abnormal, wakefulness, and would not speak of anything but Rose's boy in prison, or allow Marty, who was having coffee and reading the newspaper, when Michael began to assail him, to change the conversation to any other topic. Marty could see he had been crying. He asked Marty with an intensity Marty says he had never before seen - an intensity of eyes, of neck, of shaking legs - he asked: "Isn't there any society in the world where such things don't happen!" Marty said yes, he thought in the primitive villages, wherever they still exist, they have a better way of relating to people whose minds are different from everyone else's. They accept them there. With us, you have to be strong, or we let you die.

"They want you to die," said Michael, and he jumped up, ran into his room, clattered all the drawers, and came running out again. (By the way, it seems, from Michael's letter there's a lot Marty has not told anyone about that day...) He ran down the stairs and out the door, without another word. Marty has said that he was surprised, at the time, to see him wearing a corduroy jacket, the one he's had for years. Surprised because it was a hot day.

He wore that jacket because he needed pockets, in which to carry the gun he had recently bought, and the cartridges. The cartridge box was yellow with a black silhouette of an antelope on it, with massive antlers, and his forehead at the center of cross-hairs. When I saw it I laughed and cried at the same time. All I could remember Michael ever carrying in his pockets before, were things like pencils, pens, and newspaper clippings.

We know he went next to a place on 3rd Avenue, a methadone clinic.

About two hours after that, he checked in at the Earle Hotel, just to the west of Washington Square Park. I've been to the hotel, to see where my friend died. The door is opened by means of a buzzer pushed by the desk clerk, after he's made you stand in the light. Then you are in a narrow hallway, face-to-face with the desk man, whose seat is an old Pepsi cooler, and at your back within is the black elevator door.

I didn't want to tell this stranger anything about Michael, so I simply asked for his room - 312 - and went up there. I saw the bed, the writing desk - Was there a drop of blood on the back of the chair? It might have been blood. Other than that drop, though, you couldn't tell anything had happened in that room.

At ten o'clock, he ordered dinner sent up from a coffee shop down the block - The Chariot - and the boy who delivered his pancakes and coffee, found him sitting at the desk writing. The delivery boy later told the police Michael was anxious to get back to his writing. He grabbed the bag of food, paid, and rushed back to the table, leaving the boy to shut the door. He was writing the letter that follows, to me:

"Jack -

Greetings from the Beautiful Hotel Earle.

Here is my latest idea for a Novel - called "I Stole The Shroud of Turin."

"I STOLE THE SHROUD OF TURIN. I PUT IT UNDER MY COAT. IT BURNED MY SKIN - AS YOU HAVE READ. BUT WHAT YOU HAVE NOT READ IS THE TRUE STORY OF ALL THAT HAPPENED TO ME WHILE I HAD THAT PIECE OF CLOTH, (all I wanted was to xerox it!) AND THE POLICE WERE LOOKING FOR ME, BEFORE MY NAME WAS KNOWN TO THE WHOLE WORLD.

"THAT IS THE STORY I SHALL TELL HERE...

"HOW THREE TIMES THE SHROUD SAVED MY LIFE. AND ONCE JESUS TALKED TO ME.

"I SHALL REPORT WHAT HE SAID, AND HOW HE LOOKED & SOUNDED TO ME.

"I THANK THE *POST* FOR THIS OPPORTUNITY..."

I have been trying to call you at all the many numbers I have for you, in Baltimore, Pimlico, and surrounding areas, but none of them has connected me to you. I am willing to admit, if I had reached you, I might have been spared the necessity of the action (or would you call it a gesture?) I now see myself heading towards, because you're a man who can talk sense. How good of you, when you threatened me that time, because I was taking heroin! I had gotten my needle from my hiding place, thinking you would see the fun of it all, but you kept shaking your head, back and forth, back and forth, no matter what. You didn't care what I said. You swiped the syringe off the table-top and crushed it to bits with your shoe.

At the time I felt sorry for your small-mindedness - but now that I have crossed the territory, and it has taken my life, I see you were right.

When we first met, it was you who were considering suicide, as I recall. You were in the midst of your troubles with your parents.

We used to walk, while you discussed the necessity of leaving this earth, in order to escape the pains of life, and I presented various reasons and had emotional outbursts, attempting to convince you to wait out the bad times. I wish I could remember what I said.

Today, I was in my room, watching TV, listening to the radio, and writing, when Marty and his wife came up the stairs, home from work. With them was our friend, Louis, whom you may have met, - tall, married with a baby - lives in Long Island. Marty and I have not been talking much, largely as a result of my objections to his taking my food, and leaving whatever he doesn't take in a squashed, inedible form. I wouldn't have minded, except for my money situation. I've been waiting for a check from Brian's company, for the treatment I sent them two weeks ago, and I've been living on $10 a day.

Marty said, "I'm glad your door is open, because I want to talk to you about something important." He came to my room and sat down on the chair next to my bed. His wife and Louis followed him into the room and stood around looking at the pictures on the walls.

"All right," said Marty, "first just let me lay out all the evidence - everything I've heard about this thing - and then you answer. Tell me whether it's true or not."

"What thing?" I said.

"Well, this is it." He now spoke very rapidly, looking me straight in the eye, in what I considered to be an aggressive way, as though it were his right - his job - to search my face for signs of falsity. Then he told me several long anecdotes about the various conversations he has been having with acquaintances of mine, over the past week, to determine whether or not I was a junkie. All these anecdotes were of the form: - "So-and-so says you were unnaturally happy on such-and-such a date," or "so-and-so says you were excessively morose, on such-and-such a date." - He didn't know how to stop himself once he was started. His wife and Louis soaked it all in, in utter fascination. And, although Marty said a few times that the real purpose of all his detective work had been to learn if I needed help, "because we're ready to help you," still, after a very short time I felt like a criminal facing the D.A., and every time I said something like, "How dare you go behind my back like this?" his answer was, he had the right because a junkie will steal anything, or go crazy. This was particularly hilarious coming from Marty, who has spent time in a mental institution. When I would then object that we weren't talking about "a junkie," but me, his pal of the last fifteen years, he stated his belief that if it *was* true, and I *was* a junkie, then I wouldn't be myself, Michael Mabius, anymore, but "a junkie, capable of anything."

Therefore, the one thing of which I was not capable, was to tell him the truth. The kinds of "help" he kept talking about, he did not specify, and after a while I began to fear that what he actually did mean was that he would call the police and ask them to remove me to a secure place, where I wouldn't be bothered by drugs or any of the other temptations known to free men.

It was so strange to hear of him running around collecting evidence on me, I didn't know what to make of it. I threw them all out of the room, saying my life was none of their business. I refused to tell Marty how much, if any, dope I was taking.

When the door was closed, the whole thing got me down. I kept thinking of that line from Viet Nam - "We've got a man down! There's a man down." Then the rescue copters would flutter hacking down with stretchers, bottles, tubes for the arm, and of course, morphine... You're a man or a man down... Then a minute later I stuck my head out the door and told them all to leave my floor and go to their own. Muttering sadly, they left, taking their frightening concern with them. I felt quite estranged from my neighbors. You try to live among them, but it makes them uncomfortable. They have truly matured. They own shops. They have wives. You try to live among them, they smile, cheering you on, but they will finally drive you out. Yours is the path that leads to the wilderness, not because the wilderness loves you, but because your neighbors hate you... Marty gets his revenge, for having to admit he's a businessman. Now I see how it happens. Their fondest ideals strangle them.

I opened the window all the way, because I needed massive breathing, massive air. It felt as though my lungs had been folded for packing in a suitcase. Stone upon stone stood between myself and natural ubiquitous Oxygen. Then I leaned way out the window to see what good spying might do.

Then I had a shock. For the first time since I moved in, I was able to see people walking behind the windows of Mother Zita's Home for Friendless Women. This building has bars over the windows, and it's always dark. You never see people going in or out. Of course, once or twice I've seen the nuns - and there's a young girl who walks two dogs from there. Anyway, I've always thought the "Friendless" in the name was a way of saying the women there were pregnant, but had no husbands, and their families had kicked them out. However, today for the first time, one of the tall windows was open, and I could see the inmates of the building at their evening meal. They were dressed mostly in beltless shifts, or bathrobes, and slippers, and they had stooped shoulders - and they were mostly old, or almost old. I had thought the place was filled with pregnant girls - whom I admired, because they had decided to give birth to their babies. I think of my children, killed before their births.

But the word "Friendless." as it turns out, is not a euphemism for anything - it is the exact word. It was hard to see them, I was only able to see a leg, a foot, a long forearm hinging and unhinging as its possessor fed herself, or smoked a cigarette. I saw hair, but no faces.

Rhonda Fleming is on TV. Glenn Ford clamps a hand over her mouth so she won't scream.

This is the Second Night for Rose's boy in the Brooklyn House of Detention.

Today I was sitting at the counter inside a dark coffee shop on 23rd Street. Outside, through the plate glass window I saw a child being taken to a place on the sidewalk, and left there, alone, for a couple of minutes. This child was sitting in a tiny, narrow wheelchair. He had a very white face, with large dark eyes, that glistened as he looked around, left and right, to watch the people going by, who seemed to topple forward as they walked, pushing to their separate destinations. Some of them turned their heads, as they went, to observe him, or to return his look. He was a happy-looking little kid. What was wrong with him, that he needed the wheelchair? I couldn't tell by looking at him.

A young black man wearing a turtleneck sweater walked across the sidewalk to the wheelchair, and bent down and began tickling the child under the arms, & down the sides. The boy laughed wildly, straining every muscle to defend himself against the tickling, and meanwhile looking over the young man's shoulder, beyond him, at the people going by, to see if any of them were watching, and could see how happy he was with his friend, the man...

The man, also, was happy with the boy. You could see he was happy to be doing his job, working with crippled children, there on 23rd Street. He was proud of himself. He had the chance to be exceptional as part of his daily job, helping children. He loved his position in life. He was not alone, for he had found a family within our random mass of people... Seeing the man and the boy, you almost could have imagined that the great degradations of the last ten thousand years had never taken place. I couldn't tell if he was a teacher in the school for crippled children, or the Principal, or the bus driver who was about to take this boy and his schoolmates home. He seemed to regard the child as holy. The two of them together were from a realm of beauty, far from 23rd Street, and brought that realm, here to the street, for all those passing by, and for myself, who watched from the dark coffee-shop, to see.

Then he kissed the boy on the shiny strands of his hair, and the boy rubbed his head up against the man's chin.

Then the man went to a blue and white bus at the curb. It was a special bus, short, wide, with an iron platform, about 4 by 6 feet, that the man, by means of a set of controls in the wall of the bus, moved from its upright position to a horizontal one, and then lowered, with hydraulic dignity, to the street. The man pulled the narrow little wheelchair onto the platform and said something to the child, that made the child laugh. The man stepped off the platform, back onto the pavement, and pushed the button to raise the platform, and get the wheelchair into the bus. Inside was another man, ready to help the boy into the bus, and some other children in wheelchairs.

I watched the boy as he rose on the platform, the three feet up, and looked at the people like a king. All the solitary walkers were taken *out* of themselves, and made greater, by the single fact of the *presence* of those children on the public street, in a business area during business hours. You could see the goodness in each person going by, because of the children's presence, whereas these feelings of goodness would have been hidden, had been hidden, and would be again after they had walked twenty or thirty more steps. Except for the people who were working with the children, whose faces showed the benefits of a life of serving others, and alleviating suffering. Their faces glowed.

Some of the children had metal helmets on, signifying I know not what, while others wore knitted caps. They were all dressed very warmly, as I was, and for the same reason - because the weather report on the TV was wrong last night. Had they been dressed in their warm clothes for the trip home so they wouldn't lose their gloves or hats?

This is the best thing about this society these days - we're beginning to have crippled people with the rest of us -

I thought - this could lead to something -

All the people going by, as well as myself and the red haired waitress, seated behind the counter reading the *Post* - all of us thinking of Africa, China, Ireland, France, England, Albania, or Jerusalem - *or* Jerusalem *and* another place. These other, faraway places are our spiritual homes - the home of our shrines and origins of our religions.

Usually, we think of this city, New York, as where we do our business - even meaning by this, that our life itself is our "business" - but our reward is elsewhere - our separate rewards, in that case, *separate* us from one another. Our ideals were created in other lands, and the rewards of our living were set down for the first time in books all of languages we do not today even understand. Most of us.

But these children are not in Jerusalem, they are on 23rd Street. People are caring for these children right on 23rd Street, and in the faces of children, those taking care, and those privileged to happen upon the scene - someone being helped - they are *right now* re-creating the rewards, laws, and holy things - for this time and place.

The right of crippled people to share the streets was fought for and won in court trials. Now it has made one section of 23rd Street into what you could call a Holy Place. Even though many terrible crimes go on around the place, still it grows Holy. By bringing the crippled people out, you could *almost* think, we are taking the very first step toward turning our eyes away from Jerusalem, and the realization that Jerusalem is not our Holy Place.

It is the Holy Place for those who live in Jerusalem.

23rd Street is the new Jerusalem, and it ought to be, to worship the spirits of our own places, buildings, streets, trees, and rocks.

I immediately decided to volunteer to help these children after I'm well.

I had just learned at the methadone clinic, that they would not take me for "at least a week," since I have not got an arrest record, and when I showed their doctor the holes in my arms and legs he was extremely blase about them. He said, after all, they could have come from shooting cocaine, speed, or nothing at all. Many people, it seems, try to get on the Methadone Program without first having taken the required steps - becoming heroin addicts and reducing themselves to pennilessness. Then, casting about aimlessly for some new fascinating thrill, they decide to become methadone addicts, at the expense of Medicaid. In order to fool the Program, of course, they must start months in advance, so they will have some scars months old, some weeks old, and some recent, when they show their arms and legs to the examining physicians. "Do you really think I did that?" I asked the Doctor.

He said, "How do I know? All kinds of people come through here. I'm answerable, finally, to the State. The State checks my records. The State wants to make sure every patient has a valid reason for being on the Program."

When I discussed this problem with the Counselor, who had first sent me to the Doctor, and then saw me again after the Doctor was through with me, he said there was a way around it.

"You could be admitted immediately, if you had a record of prior treatment for drug addiction within the past two years."

I did have a record. Up till now it had not been anything to brag about, especially in polite society, but there it was - perfect for my present need - and I told the Counselor about it. "Santa Monica, California. Last August." While he tried to reach Santa Monica, the Counselor told me about himself. He said he was a poet. He's had six books published, and I have even seen some of his books in the 8th Street Bookstore (which, by the way, has been closed). Also, he himself was once a drug addict, and then was on the Program - drinking the daily vial of methadone - for nine years, before kicking it altogether.

When he told me he had taken the stuff for nine years, I became horribly depressed. When I went there, my idea was to take Methadone for less than a week - just long enough to get the heroin out of my blood - but the counselor told me that option was no longer open to those who join the Program. They found too many people went back to heroin as soon as they were bored with having nothing in them. Therefore, the State now will take you on only with the understanding you will faithfully take it for at least a year.

I thought - Let him think I'll do that. Just get some of it right now, and when you've finished yr. cartoon, and are available to suffer, just quietly walk away from the Program...

But would I get it today?

As it happened - no.

First, I couldn't remember the name of the clinic I had gone to in LA. Then, when we finally discovered it, we learned that it had been shut down by the State of California. No record of former patients available.

From then on, hope was gone. Even though the Counselor was interested in my offer to introduce him to the producers of cartoons, so he could earn extra money by writing scripts, still, he didn't feel he could overstep his authority by that much as to let me get medicated without some verification of my "previous history," as he called it. He said he would send the regular forms to the State of California and that he should receive word in a week or two.

"A week or two? Don't you care how many grocery stores I might have to hold up in that time."

He smiled. "I know exactly what you mean," he said, "These regulations are totally absurd, man, totally absurd. But what can we do?"

I went out, past the line of people waiting to "Get Medicated." They all looked tired, a little or a lot. They craned their necks to get a sight of the front of the line, where the nurses were passing plastic cups filed with yellow water out through a plastic cage. The person took his cup and filled it with orange drink from a large open vat with a spigot at the bottom, mixed the stuff with a plastic coffee-stirrer, drank it down, and then, in obedience to the rules of the Program, each one said a word or two to the Nurses. This is so the Nurses can tell they aren't trying to save any Methadone in their mouths, to spit it into a bottle, and sell it to one of the people, like me, who for some reason or other could not get Methadone legally. There were a few walking in patterns on the street in front of the Clinic door (an unmarked doorway between a Baskin-Robbins ice cream store and a pub), who were waiting for an opportunity to buy someone's supply, right out of someone's mouth, if need be...

Now my sins are all done, except for one.

Susan no longer knows me, I have not told my family anything about my recent life, and I have gradually driven the rest of the world from my corner, and now I only know the world as all the light, the vast light of all space where my dark self has no place. Therefore, I must beg your forgiveness, and I must trust that you will grant it to me. When you have read this. I will not be there to hear from your own mouth whether or not I am forgiven. I will be face-to-face with Steven, asking him why he wanted to kill me that time ten years ago, and why, when he couldn't find me, he killed himself...

It is obvious that with or without dope, (the last of which I finished 2 hours ago) - with or without pain, there is no future in this life for me, without Susan, and it is also obvious there is not the slightest chance that I will ever have her back. She is still pissed off about that time she walked in on me and that girl. I've explained how the whole thing started while I was asleep, but she won't believe me. You know. You warned me about that other girl years and years before *that*! Anyway, when you see Susan, say one last word for me. Tell her I was telling the truth. Not that it matters. Sometimes I think every story people listen to, or tell, or read, or know, is about nothing else but good luck and bad luck.

Still, there is a chance that somehow, if I keep continuing the line of words, extending the line, moving it forward, the line itself - the row of letters, with their beautiful combining variations - maybe these will pull me back into the world of the living, the continuing days, allowing me to continue among humanity. Who knows the real reason. Why so many years, nights, dawns, have found me on my side, making thousands and thousands of marks on paper? Perhaps the line knows where it is going. Or is the line through with me? Was this same line of words born long ago, and has it now grown, over the centuries, picking up and dropping individual writers along its way of progress, one day leaving each one empty while it goes on to continue its own life, complete with hidden purposes? Only now it trails out from the fingers of another writer, who is ignorant of all former writers, of the way the line is going, or why he is going with it. Now I think I should have let myself stay out among people and had my life intertwine more with other lives. I might have had more strength on this day. Perhaps coming from some other person. Even from my best friends I'm very far away. By the way, do you remember

David B. He came from Wisconsin. The last time I saw him he was collecting pieces of a brick road they were tearing up. He had bought a rundown row-house, and was restoring it. He explained how I could do the same thing. Then, when I had the house restored, it would be worth a lot more money, and I could sell it, and repeat the process with a larger house, and so on, pyramiding my profits. Since then, I've heard of people succeeding by doing that. I hope David was one of them.

Now it's almost dawn. The first thing we see is the molecular blue apparition of everything, then come the things themselves.

I once wrote a treatment about the subject of the Life-After-Death. Two scientists invent a kind of glass vacuum tank wherein the dimly outlined figures of people who have died are able to make themselves seen and heard. The result, after many montages of crowds running, is that the world once again is forced to see how helpful it is to ask one's ancestors for advice. This idea was so popular I sold it three times under different names. For the speeches in which the Dead tell what their world is like, I did a lot of reading, but there was really nothing to read. It was all too vague. I am going to a place that has never been adequately described...

I wish I could talk to Susan, but I can't call her now. She's still probably in bed, with her husband. So many years I've known her - first completely true, for year after year, then I was false, and now we are both false, like mechanisms caught in gravity and losing our ability to keep honest time.

I am a dead man now. My books have not been written, my children have not been born, or if they have, they know me not, but I am a dead man today. I haven't felt so alive in ten years, but today I am dead.

Jack, take that money out of the tree and invest it. These bad times will end... Now I'll see my Grandfather. I want to know if he's been watching me from mid-air. He'll understand what I'm doing.

It is 6:45 A.M., the 5th of July. The people are beginning to go to work. There's a woman across the street, just waking up on her couch of four green trash bags, wearing a white wig, like a judge in an English court... Look at all these people, going to work, to see if their families will rise or fall under the documents that govern us, whether they'll prosper or fall into ruin. That man in the cream-colored suit, that woman with the judge's wig, me, we all know we will be judged, finally, by these documents, and we know that after that, they will be judged by us, by what we did become, and which of the families rose, and which fell, according to what they were like.

As for me, I fell, but you can't judge the documents by me, because I put myself outside the Law, and therefore beyond the promises, and the protections, of the Law. There were times, I will say, that I stood outside the law like a hungry man outside the window of a restaurant, but it never came out to get me, and I never went in, and my death is not at the hands of the Law, nor has anyone done any wrong to me, but this is by my own hand, or God's hand, and whatever responsibility He doesn't want, I will gladly accept as my own... He brought me to a great nation, but I failed to do my part... Goodbye, Jack. -

- THE END OF MABIUS'S LETTER. -

* * *

He folded the pages of the letter in half, and put them under the cover of the top notebook in the stack of five. Then he got some sheets of newspaper and wrapped them around the notebooks. He stuffed the whole package into a brown paper bag, and addressed it to me. He sealed the package with shreds of tape. It looks like he had a single piece of tape that he tore into tiny bits, to hold as much of the package together as possible. He then removed his shoelaces and tied them around the package.

He went down the corridor and asked the maid to mail the notebooks. He gave her forty dollars, the last money he had, and asked her to take it immediately (it was almost 8 A.M.) to the 12th Street Post Office. At first, the woman was frightened by his appearance, shoeless, wearing a shirt full of holes. However, she took pity on him, because it was clear he was exhausted, and when he talked, half his words were silent, air without force. She said she would take his package to the Post Office right away.

Michael returned to the room and locked the door. He sat at the writing desk, in front of a mirror. He unwrapped his pistol from the woollen muffler in which it had been rolled up, in his jacket pocket. Holding the gun in his left hand, he aimed it at the center of his chest, and pulled the trigger. The force of the shot lifted his body out of the chair. It fell between the beds of the room. He held on to the gun. The way he fell, his hand was resting against the side of one of the beds, and the gun pointed to the ceiling. He died within two or three minutes, as the blood poured out of him. Noone reported hearing the shot, or the sound of his body falling. The same woman he had sent out with the books, returning to her job, made her rounds, and ultimately arrived at Mabius' room, and she found his body.

The funeral was on the 7th of July. He was buried side-by-side with his grandfather, on a hillside of stone monuments, covered with Hebrew and English writing, overlooking a railroad yard, where trains are painted and repaired. It is out in the country and there are branches over his head, covering him with shade. It is a beautiful place, and I know he is happy to be near his grandfather. That much I do know.

A year later, a headstone was unveiled, on which was carved,

"Michael Mabius -
1948 - 1979 -
Beloved Son,
Beloved Brother."

www.ingramcontent.com/pod-product-compliance
Lightning Source LLC
Chambersburg PA
CBHW030814310726
48980CB00006B/494/J

* 9 7 8 0 6 1 5 1 5 6 9 0 3 *